THIS
BOOK
BELONGS
TO

THE PURPLE PRINCE OF OZ

The
PURPLE PRINCE
of OZ

By

RUTH PLUMLY THOMPSON
Founded on and continuing the Famous Oz Stories

By

L. FRANK BAUM
"Royal Historian of Oz"

Illustrated by
JOHN R. NEILL

The Reilly & Lee Co.
CHICAGO

Dear Boys and Girls:

I hope you like this gay Oz adventure. Tell me if you do! It all happened about the time the June Bug came out of storage, and just about the time next year's snow balls are ripe, I'll be writing you another story.

Oz always,

RUTH PLUMLY THOMPSON.

254 S. Farragut Terrace,
West Philadelphia, Penn.

This book is cheerfully and affectionately
dedicated to

OLIVER CROMWELL CURTISS,

in less serious moments, my Big
Brother Tom. Well, there is noth-
ing serious about Oz, so cheerio,
Tom, and many merry wishes!

LIST OF CHAPTERS

CHAPTER I

Sour Grapes

"WHO is this boy?" wheezed the King of Pumperdink fretfully. "What has he done? Speak up, General, can't you see I have a headache?" Groaning a little, for he had eaten twenty pickled eggs for breakfast and found them highly indigestible, Pompus stared petulantly at the shabby boy who had just been dragged into his presence. "Who are you?" he demanded, pointing his fat finger crossly at the culprit.

"A runaway!" panted the Royal Gardener, shaking his rake.

"A thief!" added General Quakes grimly. "He has eaten all the grapes on your Majesty's favorite grape vine."

"Ugh!" winced the King, for the very thought of eating anything made him feel terribly terrible!

"Tell his Highness why you stole the grapes," ordered the general, giving the prisoner a little prod.

"Because I was hungry," answered the boy, jerking away from his two captors and staring calmly at the King.

"Hungry?" Pompus, who was really extremely soft-hearted, looked distressed. "Dear, dear, that is too bad! Well, how did you find them?"

"Sour," answered the prisoner shortly. "Very sour."

"Sour? My imperial Pumperdinkian purple grapes sour? Dip him! Dip him in the well! Take him away!" shouted Pompus, annoyed and insulted.

"What's all this noise?" murmured a sleepy voice, and Kabumpo, the Elegant Elephant, who had been enjoying his morning nap, thrust his huge head through the curtain in back of the King's throne. "Why all this excitement so early in the day?"

"This miserable little runaway has eaten the King's best grapes," explained General Quakes, rattling his sword dangerously.

"Not only that. He says they are sour!" frowned Pompus, blowing out his cheeks and rolling his eyes indignantly around at the Elegant Elephant.

"Sour grapes! Ho, ho! Kerumph!" rumbled Kabumpo, coming all the way out. "Told you so right to your face? Well, there's courage for you. What's your name, young one?"

"Randy," answered the prisoner, glancing curiously up at the gorgeously caparisoned elephant.

"Randy what?" yawned Kabumpo.

"Just Randy." Thrusting both hands in his pockets, the boy, who was about ten with black hair and eyes, looked composedly at his captors.

"Well, I'll Randy him," fumed Pompus, clasping his hands on his stomach. "Dip him three times and return him to his family at once!"

"Where are you from?" roared General Quakes, seizing Randy's arm. But at this, Randy closed his mouth tight and refused to speak; and though the gardener on one side and the general on the other continued to shake and question, not a word could they get out of him.

19

"I saw him sneaking down from the mountains last evening," insisted the gardener testily. "He must live in the mountains. Where do you belong, you little grape eater, you?"

"Stop!" trumpeted Kabumpo indignantly, as Randy

was jerked first by one arm and then the other. "Do you want to pull the boy in two? I, myself, will take this lad for an attendant. Spezzle is old and anxious to retire, so let me have this boy, your Majesty, and I promise he shall never bother you again. Will you come with me and do exactly as I say?" asked the

Elegant Elephant, squinting down his trunk at the shabby little Gilliken. Randy looked dubiously up into Kabumpo's snapping little eyes, but detecting an unmistakable wink, thankfully nodded his head.

"Then take him away at once. Take him away!" ordered Pompus, clapping both hands to his aching middle. "Can't you see I'm suffering? Go away, all of you!"

"How about the dipping?" sniffed the gardener, who felt that the prisoner was getting off far too easily.

"I'll attend to that," answered the Elegant Elephant haughtily, and picking Randy up in his trunk he tossed him lightly to his shoulder and stalked with great dignity from the purple throne room.

Now Pumperdink, as many of you already know, is an old-fashioned Oz Kingdom way up in the northern part of the Gilliken Country, its royal family being one of the oldest and most interesting in Oz. Pompus, the King, rules over his subjects with great ease and cleverness. All who obey the laws are rewarded; all who break the laws are promptly dipped in the royal well. As the well water is purple and dyes offenders as thoroughly and effectively as we dye Easter Eggs, and as the dye sticks for almost

21

two weeks, the Pumperdinkians are very careful not to break the laws, so that revolutions or uprisings are practically unknown in that pleasant and peaceful valley. It is not often that Pompus loses his temper, either—only when he eats pickled eggs. Usually he is the kindest and most considerate of monarchs. Indeed, Pompus and Pozy Pink, his Queen, are famed far and wide for their cheerfulness and generosity.

As for Pompadore, the King's son, and his Princess, Peg Amy, and their little daughter Pajonia, *they* make life in the purple castle so delightfully interesting and jolly that I can think of no happier place to live or visit. No wonder Kabumpo prefers Pumperdink to any other kingdom in the realm. And speaking of Kabumpo I had better explain at once that the Elegant Elephant was given to Pompus simply Oz ages ago by a famous Blue Emperor. And Kabumpo has shown himself so wise and sagacious, has lent such style and elegance to the Court that he has been made a member of the royal family with the rank of Prince and Chancellor.

The King confers with Kabumpo on every occasion and matter of importance and would not think of undertaking a journey or war without first consulting his Elegant Elephant. Which, of course, only proves that Kabumpo is no ordinary pachyderm. No, Kabumpo is the largest elephant in Oz and in that strange and exciting country where animals can talk as well and sometimes better than their masters, it is no small honor to be the greatest animal of all.

Kabumpo sees and does things in a big way and if he is a bit haughty and proud with lesser folk, who can blame him? His heart, when you get right down to it, is in exactly the right place and beats warmly and loyally for his King and country. It was this same big heart that prompted the Elegant Elephant to come to the aid of the mountain boy, and he had no intention at all of dipping Randy in the purple well. Once back in his huge and comfortable apartment on the first floor of the palace, Kabumpo gave him food, new clothes and a long lecture on court etiquette. But the lecture was so mixed with jokes and funny stories that Randy did not mind it at all and by evening was beginning to feel perfectly at ease and at home in the grand and sumptuous quarters of the Elegant Elephant of Oz.

"As good a place as any to begin," he sighed, snuggling comfortably down in the soft bed Kabumpo had ordered the palace servants to place in the enormous dressing room. "As good a place as any. Ho, hum, I wonder how long it will take me!"

CHAPTER 2

A Strange Story

THE Elegant Elephant was dressing for dinner. Kabumpo always dressed for dinner, wearing his costliest jewels and most elaborately embroidered robes of state as became a member of the royalest family in Oz. As he surveyed himself calmly and leisurely in the glass, Kabumpo was turning over in his mind some stories that might amuse little Princess Pajonia and keep her quiet and happy during the long tedious dinner hour.

"I'll tell her the tale of the pink goat," decided the Elegant Elephant, taking up a small mirror in his trunk and examining himself critically from all sides. "Just pull that robe a bit to the right, Randy, and see that the buckle is caught, will you?" Randy, perched on a tall ladder beside Kabumpo, gave a little sniff of impatience, but carefully straightened the velvet robe, fastened the jeweled buckle and then, resting his elbows on his knees, stared gloomily into the long mirror. "That's it," approved Kabumpo, paying no attention to Randy's sulky expression. "You grow handier every day, my boy. Why, soon you'll be the handiest attendant I ever have had." Randy said nothing, but sniffed again, this time quite audibly.

"Now what's the matter?" grunted Kabumpo, looking at him sharply. "Many a lad would think it an honor to wait upon the Elegant Elephant of Oz. Have you not a fine bed, new clothes and all you want to eat? Haven't I taken you riding when no one was about, and allowed you to play marbles with my best earrings? And who was it, pray, who saved you from being sent home in disgrace? Who made a place for you in the King's household so you could see something of high life? And now you sit there

and sniff at me. Hem! Ho! Kerumph!" Snorting
with displeasure, Kabumpo glared at Randy, and
Randy without explanation or apology glared back.
But for all his independence and sauciness, there was
something extremely likeable about this little Gilliken and though he showed no proper deference or
respect for Kabumpo's rank and position, the Elegant Elephant already felt an unaccountable liking
and affection for him. Still, it was unthinkable that
any one fortunate enough to associate with an elephant as important and grand as himself should be
discontented or unhappy. Kabumpo just couldn't
understand it.

"You ought to be ashamed of yourself," he grumbled, shaking his trunk sternly at his little attendant. "What's the matter with you, anyway?"

"Oh, nothing," sighed Randy, running nimbly down
the ladder. "Nothing's the matter. That's just it.
Nothing! Nothing ever happens here." Folding his
arms Randy looked scornfully out over the quiet and
serene gardens of the castle.

"Nothing ever happens here!" exclaimed Kabumpo,
coming round with one majestic sweep. "How do
you know nothing happens? You've been here only
a week. Let me tell you, my lad, things have hap-

27

pened in Pumperdink that would make your ears flap and your chin quiver. Things that would curl up your knees and your nose, young one!"

"Really!" Randy tried to speak indifferently but could not keep the interest out of his voice; Kabumpo, pulling an enormous gold watch from a pocket in his robe and seeing that there was still half an hour before dinner, demanded mysteriously:

"Have you ever heard of scroll magic?"

Randy slowly shook his head.

"Ha, I thought not. Well, Randy, if it had not been for scroll magic, Prince Pompadore would never have married, Princess Peg Amy would still be a wooden doll and I should never have visited the Emerald City of Oz. It began on just such a day as this," confessed the Elegant Elephant, looking uneasily out of the window, "just such a day as this. Pompa's birthday it was, too, and when we blew out the candles on the birthday cake, the cake itself exploded and knocked us all about. And when we picked ourselves up, there was this scroll saying that if Prince Pompadore did not marry a proper princess in a proper span of time, Pumperdink would disappear forever, and even longer, from the Gilliken Country of Oz. Think of that, my boy!"

Without much enthusiasm Randy thought of that and Kabumpo, warming to his tale, hurried on: "Well, after the first shock of the scroll the King and the Prime Pumper decided to marry Pompa to Faleero, who happens to be the only princess around here."

"That old witch we saw gathering faggots yesterday?" gasped Randy in a shocked voice. "Why, she's as old as Stone Mountain!"

"Older!" rasped Kabumpo, shaking his head angrily at the mere memory of the thing. "And, you know, the King and Pumper were so set on saving the Kingdom at once that I had to run off with Pompa to rescue him from the awful old creature."

"Well, what happened then?" asked Randy, edging closer and beginning to play with the fringe on Kabumpo's robe.

"Pl—enty!" rumbled the Elegant Elephant, shifting from one foot to the other. "Pompa and I traveled all over Oz to find a proper princess and not only found her and saved Pumperdink from disappearing but rescued Ozma and her courtiers from a giant, as well." The Elegant Elephant tried to look modest as he made this statement, but he did not succeed very well and, as Randy was now all ears,

29

he told with great earnestness and enjoyment the whole story of Peg Amy's enchantment and Prince Pompadore's strange adventures and marriage.

"It all began when an old wizard named Glegg fell in love with the young and beautiful Princess of Sun Top Mountain," explained Kabumpo, with a huge sigh. "Consulting his book of the future, Glegg discovered that the princess was to marry Prince Pompadore of Pumperdink. To prevent this he sent the threatening scroll, hoping to frighten Pompa into a marriage with some other princess. See?" Randy nodded quickly. "But when Glegg asked the princess to marry him, of course she refused, and in a fit of anger he turned her into a little tree in Ozma's garden. Believing she would tire of this enchantment and finally consent to marry him, Glegg hid his box of magic in a cave under Ozma's castle and set himself to wait for the princess to change her mind. But what happened?" Kabumpo lifted his trunk scornfully. "Cap'n Bill, an old sailor who lives in the Emerald City, wishing to surprise Trot, a little mortal girl who lives with Ozma, cut down the tree and carved a wooden doll from the wood. Trot, never knowing her doll had been a princess, called her Peg Amy and dressed her and loved her and carried her every place she went. Then, Ruggedo, the old Gnome King, who had been banished from his own dominions, took refuge in Glegg's cave, found his box of mixed magic and almost destroyed the Emerald City."

"But what about the wooden doll?" begged Randy, trying to piece all these strange incidents together.

"Tut, tut! I'm coming to that," puffed Kabumpo, glancing hurriedly at his watch. "Ruggedo stole the doll, my boy, and took her to his cave. He wanted somebody to scold and shake. He had already hired a rabbit, named Wag, to wait upon him but Wag would not allow the Gnome King even to box his ears, so Ruggedo shook and scolded Peg to his heart's content, pretending she was Kaliko, his old steward. Fortunately Peg could not feel and Wag, the rabbit, took as good care of her as he could. Now, soon after stealing Peg, Ruggedo found Glegg's box of magic containing Spike's hair strengthener, expanding fluid, reanimating rays, some trick tea, and many other powerful salves and appliances. Wishing to be as strong as possible, Ruggedo poured the hair strengthener on his head. It instantly turned his hair into long iron spikes. Then, wishing to try the expanding fluid, he poured a little on Wag, the rabbit, while he was asleep, and on the wooden doll. Immediately they grew as large as you are and when he tried the reanimating rays on Peg she came to life and chased Rug all over the cavern."

"Well, good for her!" exclaimed Randy. "Did she catch him?"

"No," admitted Kabumpo ruefully, "for Ruggedo, afraid Peg would pay him back for all the shakings, poured all the rest of the expanding fluid over himself. First he expanded east and west till he filled the whole cavern and next he shot up as tall as a giant, bursting through the top of the cave. Then, with Ozma's castle caught on the spikes of his head like a crown, the Gnome King stepped out of the cave, tramped off to Ev and sat down on a mountain.

And here's where *we* come in," announced Kabumpo impressively. "I had about decided that Ozma was the proper princess for Pompa to marry, and right after Ruggedo disappeared with the castle, we arrived in the Emerald City. Almost immediately we met Wag and Peg. They had escaped from the cave and with Glegg's box of mixed magic were on their way to find the Gnome King, who they felt sure meant to destroy Ozma and her courtiers. We naturally determined to go with them and though the wooden doll did not know she was a princess and we did not know it either, we liked her at once and grew fonder of her all the time. Well—" Kabumpo, taking another look at his watch, hurriedly continued the story, "—after some breath-taking adventures we finally reached Ev and with the help of Glegg's magic, forced Ruggedo to march back to the Emerald City. Once there, he resumed his natural size and shape; the castle was restored to its foundations and the Gnome King himself was banished to a lonely island in the Nonestic Ocean. But Ozma refused to marry Prince Pompadore and when we asked Glegg's question box who was the proper princess it told us to go to Sun Top Mountain. So, weary and discouraged though we were, we traveled on to Sun Top Mountain, taking Wag and Peg Amy along. When we reached the castle, the princess, of course, was not there, but no sooner had Peg Amy crossed the threshold, than the enchantment of Glegg was broken, and she became her own charming self. As she and Pompadore were very much in love they were married on the spot. Then we all returned to Pumperdink and have been here ever since; little Princess Pajonia was born four years ago last February. Is it all clear now?"

"About as clear as custard," sniffed Randy. "And has nothing happened since, sir?"

"Well, nothing so exciting as all that," admitted Kabumpo slowly, "but one never can tell, one never can tell when something will happen again." The Elegant Elephant was extremely pleased to have Randy address him as "sir." It was the first time the boy had done so.

"He'll do!" chuckled Kabumpo delightedly, under his breath. "He'll do! How would you like to go into dinner with me?" he added aloud, and before Randy could answer, tossed him lightly to his shoulder. "Now for haysake," he cautioned gruffly, "for haysake, speak when you are spoken to and try to remember you are in the presence and on the back of Royalty." Randy, seated comfortably on Kabumpo's broad back, smothered his chuckles in the Elegant Elephant's velvet robe and Kabumpo billowed slowly and majestically down the gold-paved hallway to the royal banquet hall of the King.

35

CHAPTER 3

The Mist Tree

NOW Randy had not seen the royal family of Pumperdink since he had been caught by General Quakes and dragged into the throne room, and as Kabumpo swept grandly into the great dining hall the boy felt extremely nervous and uneasy. He was not sure that the King would be pleased to see him again, so he made himself as small as possible and peered inquisitively and anxiously over the Elegant Elephant's left ear.

36

"Oyez! Oyez! Way for the Elegant Elephant of Oz,
Three bows and three bumps for Kabumpo!"

cried the Prime Pumper of the Realm, pounding
three times on the floor with his golden staff. At
this, all the courtiers bowed their heads three times
and tapped three times on the table with their
knives. The royal family did not bow but nodded
graciously as the Elegant Elephant took his place
behind the King's chair. The baby princess clapped
her hands with glee and Pompa immediately leaned
over to whisper to Kabumpo a joke he had just heard
from the gardener. The long table twinkled with
candles in golden holders and glittered with gold and
silver dishes. Twenty footmen in white wigs and
purple satin uniforms served a succession of savory
viands to the brilliantly clad and royal company and
no one noticed Randy at all.

Everything, in fact, was so carefree and jolly that
he stopped worrying and began to enjoy himself.
It was hard to believe that the lovely Princess of
Pumperdink had once been a wooden doll, and regarding her solemnly Randy tried to imagine how
she must have looked and felt during that strange
enchantment. The Queen of Pumperdink was lovely,
too, and seemed scarcely old enough to have a son

as tall as Pompadore. The Prince, on his part, looked exactly as Randy wished to look himself when he was grown, and after a long approving scrutiny—during which he decided to be as nearly like him as possible, to marry a princess as lovely as Peg Amy and have a little daughter as pretty as Pajonia—he turned his attention to the other members of the King's family and household.

Pompus, very fat and gorgeous in pearl-studded velvet, was seated at the head of the table. Beside him was a thin, sly-looking fellow whom he addressed as Kettywig. Randy was just wondering who he might be when Kabumpo, who had been telling Pajonia a story, called out in his booming voice:

"Well, Brother Kettywig, how are you enjoying your stay in our castle and kingdom?"

" 'Brother'!" gasped Kettywig, throwing down his napkin and turning angrily to the King. "Are you going to sit there and allow that great beast to call me 'brother'?"

"Oh, bosh and bother, now, what's the difference?" muttered Pompus, popping a whole biscuit into his mouth. "You are my brother, aren't you? Well, Kabumpo wants to make you feel at home. It's just his little joking way, you know."

"*Little* joking way!" sputtered Kettywig. "There's nothing little about the creature but his wits. Make me feel at home, indeed! How could I feel at home in a country where an elephant calls me 'brother'?" Choking with indignation, Kettywig seized a goblet of water and swallowed it down at one gulp.

"You wouldn't feel at home anywhere but a pickle factory," sniffed the Elegant Elephant, taking a platter of hot chicken from a footman and calmly passing it back to Randy. "Or in a mustard mine!" he finished scornfully. "Hah!" Randy almost held his breath at such audacity, but the King, after a wink at his favorite, went quietly on with his dinner, leaving Kettywig to recover himself as best he could. The royal orchestra had meanwhile struck up a lively tune so that further conversation was impossible and Randy, making short work of the chicken and candied fruit Kabumpo passed him from time to time, settled back with a little sigh of content. And when, a few moments later, a page ran in to announce that a traveling magician was without and desired to entertain the company, Randy's interest and satisfaction knew no bounds.

"And what is he without, pray?" inquired Kabumpo, as the King thoughtfully rubbed his chin.

"He says he is without a peer, sir," stuttered the page, casting uneasy glances over his shoulder.

"How can a magician without a peer appear?" demanded Kabumpo argumentatively.

"What nonsense!" roared Pompus setting down his tumbler. "Tell the fellow to come in, Pantleg. I, for one, would like to see a magician without a peer appear." Hearing Pompus' command and without waiting to be announced, the magician, with a long, lightning-like slide, shot into the banquet hall, coming to a neat stop beside the King's chair.

"Nishibis, the Wiz—ard!" piped Pantleg, jumping

behind a pillar. As Nishibis bowed deeply right and left, Randy stood up to get a better look at the fellow. He was thin, shriveled up and ugly, his face almost hidden by dark spectacles and a peaked cap. Over his shoulder he carried a blue bag of tricks, and his voice when he spoke was high and irritating.

"Now, where have I heard that voice before?" thought Randy, as Nishibis drew a yellow scarf from his sack and with strange mumbles and screeches began twirling it around his head. At the third twirl, the scarf became a small dragon. Spreading its wings it flew straight for little Princess Pajonia, and as she drew back in alarm it melted into a small yellow kitten that nestled cozily in her arms.

"Bravo! Bravo!" cried Kettywig, and even Kabumpo looked pleased and curious. Next the magician pulled a bundle of twigs from the bag. Taking a candle from the table he set them afire and tossed them high in the air. A pleasant blue smoke floated through the banquet hall and presently the spirals formed into a tall blue mist tree that hung in the air directly before the King.

"A magic flower for his Majesty and his Majesty's family," announced Nishibis. And sure enough, five fiery red roses were blooming on the wizard's tree.

"You have forgotten me!" snorted Kabumpo indignantly. "Is your magic not strong enough to tell you that I, too, am a member of the King's family?"

"A rose for an elephant! Ha, ha!" jeered Kettywig. "Make it a cabbage, my good wizard." While Kabumpo glared and Pompus looked embarrassed, Nishibis shrugged his shoulders.

"My magic grows roses only for Royalty," he explained insolently. "And if your Highnesses will pluck these flowers, a great good fortune will befall."

"Probably scorch our fingers," observed Prince Pompadore, who did not care much for magic, having had some disagreeable experiences with it.

"Oh, come on, let's pick them," begged Peg Amy eagerly, and as the King and Queen were equally curious to know what would happen, they all leaned forward and each picked a rose, even little Princess Pajonia. As the five stems snapped, there were five sharp explosions and Randy, leaping to his feet, saw the mist tree dissolving into a thick black cloud. But of the King and his family he saw nothing. They had vanished with the wizard's roses, and confronted by five empty chairs, the courtiers of Pumperdink gasped with fright and consternation.

"A great good fortune has befallen. Ha, ha!

Ha, ha!" croaked the magician, and whirling round and round he swung his blue bag over his head.

"Good fortune? Good fortune? For whom?" screeched Kabumpo, lashing his trunk back and forth and swaying like a ship in a storm.

"For Kettywig!" shouted Nishibis, pointing to Pompus' brother, who had risen and was facing the company with great composure. "Kettywig is next in succession. Ketty is KING! The King is dead, long live the King!"

"Nothing of the kind!" trumpeted Kabumpo. "The King has only disappeared. Bring him back at once, you miserable, meddling, magic-working monster! Treason! Treeson—mist treeson!" boomed the Elegant Elephant at the top of his trunk. At his mighty cries, General Quakes and the royal guards burst through the doorway, all the courtiers jumped to their feet and a scene of the utmost confusion ensued. Only Kettywig remained calm. As the guards, moving forward none too willingly, attempted to seize the wizard, Kettywig spoke:

"Stop!" commanded the King's brother, in a commanding voice. "I am now your ruler. From now on you take orders from me. Understand?"

"Oyez! Oyez! I hereby pronounce Kettywig King

43

of Pumperdink," quavered the Prime Pumper in a feeble voice.

"Oyez! Oyez, you *would* say that to save your silly neck." Snatching the old statesman into the air

Kabumpo shook him violently to and fro. "How dare you call this pitiful plotter King?" Turning to the cowering courtiers he roared in a loud voice: "Rise up! Rise up, and force these impostors to restore our rightful rulers!"

"The first one who touches me shall vanish!" warned Nishibis, showing his yellow teeth and scowling so horribly that the guards fell back in horror; and when Kabumpo himself lunged forward, Randy tugged him frantically by the ear.

"Be careful! Be careful!" begged the little boy in an earnest voice. "If you disappear, who is to help the King?"

"Remove that elephant!" commanded Kettywig, pounding on the table with his fist. "Remove him, dip him, put him in irons!"

"I'll attend to him," hissed the wizard, and as the guards made a half-hearted motion toward their old friend, Kabumpo, Nishibis snatched a second bundle of twigs from his sack and lighting them hurled the blazing circlet straight at the Elegant Elephant's head. But he had not counted on Randy. Leaning forward the little Gilliken neatly caught the blazing bundle and before they could take effect hurled them straight back. Now Randy had aimed at Nishibis, but in the extreme hurry and excitement of the moment he overshot his mark and the hissing, crackling bundle fell straight upon the head of Pumper, who melted away before their eyes, leaving nothing but his gold staff and spectacles. Yes,

45

the King's chief adviser was now as gone as the King of Pumperdink himself.

Before the company recovered from the shock, before the guards could take another step, the Elegant Elephant threw up his trunk and with a bellow

of rage that blew out all the candles charged furiously from the banquet hall, never stopping till he reached his own apartment. The guardsmen, urged into action by dishes, cups, plates and spoons flung by Kettywig, were not far behind and as Kabumpo rushed into his own quarters Randy heard the door slam and two iron bolts slip into place. Next all the shutters were banged to from the outside and heavy feet pounded up and down the passageways.

"Well!" panted the Elegant Elephant, leaning wearily against the wall, "I suppose now, my boy, you are satisfied. Something has happened, something *has* happened at last. Ugh! Ahhh! Why didn't I disappear and go out with the people I care for instead of staying here with these frightened fools and cowards?"

"Don't you like me at all?" asked Randy in a small voice. Kabumpo, suddenly recollecting Randy's bravery, cleared his throat apologetically.

"Of course I like you," he answered gruffly. "I like you a lot. Didn't you save me from vanishing? But what good will it do?" he gulped in the next breath. "My whole family has been wiped out and the throne stolen by a couple of plotting rascals. What can I do against magic?"

"Well, you did something before," Randy reminded him quickly. "You saved the whole kingdom from disappearing."

"But last time we were only threatened. This time everybody has actually vanished."

47

"You haven't," persisted Randy, shuddering a little as a loud scream echoed along the corridor.

"That's so!" mused Kabumpo thoughtfully. "That's so!" His eyes began to twinkle and snap with excitement. "I'm still here and I'll fool them yet. I did something before and I'll do it again. We'll get out of the country at once, find some magic and return, and then let King Kettywig see who is strongest!"

"But we're locked in," whispered Randy anxiously.

"Are we?" Sniffing scornfully, Kabumpo lifted Randy to the floor and began to make hasty preparations for departure. Into a small leather bag he put the largest and most valuable of his jewels and donned his darkest and sturdiest robe. Giving Randy a small jeweled sword that had once been Prince Pompa's, he bade him lie down and get a little rest. Randy buckled on the sword but was far too excited to sleep. The castle was growing quieter and as the great clock in the tower tolled one, Kabumpo touched Randy on the shoulder. The boy wondered how they would get out without waking the guards, but he did not wonder long. Kabumpo, after a few whispered instructions, lifted Randy up to the glass transom over the door. While the Elegant Elephant held him by the heels he cleverly slipped back the bolts. Then, without a sound and without encountering a single guard, Kabumpo trod softly down the golden hallways and slipped out through a side door of the castle.

CHAPTER 4

In Follensby Forest

THE night was dark and moonless and Kabumpo sped like a flying cloud through the silent city and sleeping villages of Pumperdink. Then, leaving the King's Highway, he turned east into the tangled forest domain of Faleero, the old and ugly princess whom Pompa had so nearly been forced to marry. In the center of the forest the Elegant Elephant stopped, and wrapping Randy in an old robe he had brought along for the purpose urged him to sleep until morning.

"No one will look for us here," yawned Kabumpo, leaning wearily against a giant oak, and before the boy had time to answer he was asleep and snoring so tremendously that leaves fell in perfect showers upon Randy's upturned face and a family of squirrels in the hollow trunk fled for their lives. For nearly an hour the boy lay thinking of the strange happenings in Pumperdink. He wondered curiously how it felt to disappear and where he had heard the magician's voice before. While he was trying to remember he, too, fell asleep and dreamed he was flying on a yellow dragon to the Emerald City of Oz. A great rustle and splash wakened him next morning, and rolling out of Kabumpo's old robe he saw the Elegant Elephant vigorously bathing in a shallow forest stream. The sun was shining somewhere up above, but the trees were so close together that only a pale green light came flickering down into the forest.

"Want a shower?" inquired Kabumpo cheerfully, and as Randy joined him he sent a spray of water high into the air.

"No thank you, sir." Shivering a little, Randy,

who was no fonder of washing than most boys, dashed a little water on the tip of his nose and dipping his fingers into the icy water hastily wiped them on his handkerchief.

"Now, don't call me 'sir'," blustered Kabumpo, giving himself a shake that sent water spraying in

every direction. "We're just comrades from now on, my boy, comrades in misfortune. Anyone brave enough to catch a wizard's bundle of tricks, needn't call anyone 'sir.' Hah!" Expelling his breath in a great whistle, Kabumpo beamed on Randy, and

Randy, blushing with pleasure at such praise, beamed back.

"Do you really think I am brave?" asked the boy.

Kabumpo nodded vigorously. "But why do you ask me that?" he went on conversationally. "Do you especially want to be brave?"

"It's awfully important to be brave," answered Randy, brushing back his thick hair. "Don't you think so, Kabumpo?"

"Well," mused Kabumpo, rubbing himself briskly with a bunch of leaves, "if you are an important person you ought to be brave, but if you're not, I can't see that it makes much difference. But I do think," the Elegant Elephant stopped rubbing and looked sharply at Randy, "I do think you should tell me a bit more about yourself, and I am not at all sure you should accompany me on this journey. No telling what may happen. And after all it is not your affair, but mine, to save the Kingdom of Pumperdink."

"Oh, don't say that," begged Randy, throwing his arm around Kabumpo's trunk. "You helped me. Now let me help you. Please! Please!"

"But what about your family?" demanded Kabumpo. "You really should go home, you know."

"Not yet! Not yet!" pleaded the boy, tightening his hold on the Elegant Elephant's trunk. "I want to see all of Oz before I do that."

"M-mmm!" mumbled the Elegant Elephant, beginning to weaken. "Well, it will do you no harm to see a little of the country, but it's my guess you are no common mountain boy, used to goats and goatherds. You have too much style for that." Randy grinned a little at this, and, as Kabumpo had finished drying himself, he climbed into a tree and helped him adjust his grey velvet traveling cloak. Then, as they were both by this time terribly hollow, they began to look around for something to eat. The Elegant Elephant breakfasted quite comfortably on several barrels of leaves, but Randy had to satisfy himself with a cake of chocolate Kabumpo had slipped into his pocket the night before.

"Where are we going first?" inquired the boy as Kabumpo, having eaten all the leaves he could hold, lifted him carefully aloft.

"I—don't—know—," admitted Kabumpo, picking his way cleverly between the tall trees. "I thought of going straight to the Emerald City and appealing to Ozma and the Wizard of Oz for help. The practice of magic, as you know, is forbidden in Oz, and

Ozma would not only punish this meddling magician but force him to restore the King and his family at once. On the other trunk," the Elegant Elephant cleared his throat self consciously, "I'd much rather rescue the royal family myself."

"Oh, so should I!" agreed Randy, with an understanding nod. "But how are we going to do it?"

"Search me!" Kabumpo flapped his ears, crushing twigs and branches wrathfully under his feet. "I never liked Kettywig from the moment he set foot in the palace. He must have planned to steal Pompus' throne from the very beginning, and s-a-y how I wish you'd caught that villain with his own magic, though putting Pumper out of the way was a big help. The very idea of him calling Kettywig 'King' just to save his own silly neck. The very *idea*!"

"I wonder what he's doing now," called Randy, lying flat on Kabumpo's back to escape the scratching of the overhanging twigs and branches.

"Pretending to be King," sniffed the Elegant Elephant, lifting his trunk with huge scorn. "He's just a pretender pretending to his business. Hah! Wait till I get my trunk on the fellow!" Increasing his pace, Kabumpo went crashing through the underbrush, too angry for further speech, and presently

55

they came to an irregular clearing in the forest. At the furthest end stood a small, mean-looking hut.

"Who lives here?" inquired Randy, sitting up curiously as Kabumpo came to a sudden stop.

"Faleero!" answered Kabumpo, speaking quietly out of the corner of his mouth. "The Fairy Princess of Follensby Forest. Shall we drop in and pay our respects, my boy?"

"Not unless you want to," chuckled Randy, for the last time they had seen Faleero she had not only tried to hit them with a bundle of nettles, but had screeched so loud and fearsomely that the Elegant Elephant had taken to his heels.

"Well," snickered Kabumpo, "I, myself, have no desire to see her hideous old Highness, but if she is out, we might find some food in the royal hovel. Anyway let's have a look." In spite of his great size Kabumpo could move without a sound, and stepping softly to the back window, he and Randy peered in.

"Why, there's Nishibis!" shuddered Randy, grasping his sword.

"Sh—hh!" warned Kabumpo, pressing closer to the window. It was strange enough to find the rascally magician in Faleero's hut, but as the two looked anxiously through the glass an even stranger thing

PRESENTLY THEY CAME TO AN IRREGULAR CLEARING

happened. Snatching off his peaked hat and spectacles and clapping his bony hands together, Nishibis gave three piercing screeches. Immediately three bent old crones hobbled briskly into the room. The first took the wizard's cloak, the second pulled off

the wizard's beard, the third tossed his blue bag into the corner, and the wizard, no longer a wizard but a wizened and ancient old lady, began to hop, skip and prance in crazy circles, yelling at the top of her cracked and disagreeable voice:

"Drink to my happiness, drink, oh, drink,
For I'm to be Queen of Pumperdink!
Dance to my happiness, dance and jig;
Faleero shall marry King Kettywig!"

"Faleero!" gulped Kabumpo, clapping his trunk to his forehead as the four old witches continued to dance and caper about in the firelight.

"No wonder I knew that wizard's voice," exclaimed Randy. "Remember the day she chased us, Kabumpo? Why, she just pretended to be a magician!"

"But she certainly knows her magic! Great Grump! Just look at the old fury! She and Kettywig must have planned this from the very first. Well, I wish him joy of his bargain. What a queen! What a king! What a mix-up!"

"Who are those other old women?" queried Randy, pressing his nose against the glass.

"Ladies in waiting to her Majesty," answered Kabumpo, with a little sniff.

"They look as if they had been waiting a long time," said Randy, lowering his head cautiously. "Are we going in?"

"Not in, on," said Kabumpo grimly, "on and on and—on, till we're entirely out of this mischievous forest. No use tackling Faleero without any magic," and swinging noiselessly away from the Royal Hut, Kabumpo plunged again into the deep and impenetrable forest.

"Faleero's been furious ever since Pompa married Peg Amy," confided the Elegant Elephant, shouldering his way through a dense tangle of vines and underbrush. "But I never thought she would do us any actual harm. I tell you, my boy, it's a dangerous thing to offend a fairy, especially an old fairy."

"She doesn't seem much like a fairy to me," sighed Randy, settling himself comfortably between the Elegant Elephant's ears. "But then, I suppose there are bad fairies as well as good ones." Kabumpo mournfully agreed that there were. Then, lifting his trunk, he suddenly came to a complete standstill.

"Someone's coming," he announced uneasily. Randy could not hear a sound and was about to tell Kabumpo he must surely be mistaken, when a tall weird figure in a dark cloak sprang out of the gloom.

"Sooth! Sooth! Sooth!" cried the stranger, in a loud and challenging voice. "Sooth! Sooth! Sooth!"

"Why do you cry 'sooth'?" rumbled the Elegant Elephant irritably.

"Because I am a soothsayer," stated the fellow, extending both arms. "Sooth! Sooth! Sooth!"

"Oh, bother such stuff and nonsense!" exclaimed Kabumpo, swaying irritably to and fro. "If you have anything to soothsay, for Grump's sake say it! We are in a hurry, a great hurry!"

"An elephant is always great, whether he hurries or not," replied the soothsayer soothingly. "And just permit me to observe that there is no door a golden key will not open."

"But there isn't any door around here," objected

Randy, leaning over to look more closely at the sooth-sayer. Kabumpo, however, seemed to understand perfectly what was wanted and was already fumbling with his trunk in the pocket of his robe.

"Here," he said, not ungraciously, holding out to the soothsayer a huge and gleaming pearl. "Unlock the doors of your soothsaying mind and tell us something really useful."

"Ah!" smiled the stranger, greedily pocketing the

jewel. "You drop pearls of wisdom when you speak. Then harken and hear ye:

"A person of high rank and extreme importance is traveling toward the Emerald City of Oz."

"Everyone around here knows me," muttered Kabumpo, in a pleased aside to Randy. "Everybody!"

"I was not referring to your royal self," sniffed the soothsayer, who had overheard Kabumpo's whisper. With a provoking wink at Randy he folded his arms and began to back away into the forest, and before the Elegant Elephant had recovered from his shock and displeasure, he spoke again.

"In the castle of the Red Jinn you will find what you seek. He, alone, can help you." As Kabumpo and Randy stared at him in utter amazement he disappeared between the trees but after a short silence his mocking voice came floating back to them:

"Step by step one goes a long way."

"Oooh! I wonder how long a way it is?" breathed Randy, looking at the spot where the soothsayer had been. "Oh, Kabumpo, do you suppose the King and his family are really in the castle of the Red Jinn? Then all we have to do is find the Red Jinn."

"But we don't even know where he is," blustered the Elegant Elephant, forgetting that he had been

63

insulted. "Still, if he's a Red Jinn—" Kabumpo began to move swiftly in the direction the soothsayer had taken. "If he's a Red Jinn his castle must be in the Quadling Country, for that is the reddest Kingdom in Oz. Everything is red there, even the bluest books." Trumpeting with pleasure at his own cleverness, Kabumpo flung forward at such a pace that Randy had all he could do to stay aboard and no breath at all to ask questions.

" 'Step by step,' did he say?" Kabumpo bellowed gleefully. "Well, here we go step by stepping!"

CHAPTER 5

The River Road

THOUGH Randy had no breath to speak, he was doing a heap of thinking as Kabumpo rushed recklessly through Follensby Forest. Like all the other boys in the wonderful Kingdom of Oz he had studied his geozify and hoztry, as they call geography and history in that merry and magical country. He knew that Oz was ruled by Ozma, a lovely girl fairy in the famous Emerald City. And although he had

65

never visited the capital himself, he knew that it was in the exact center of the Kingdom just where the four triangular countries of the realm met. The northernmost country of Oz, where Randy lived, was the Gilliken or purple country, the western dominions of Oz were the Blue Lands of the Munchkins. To the east lay the yellow Winkie Kingdom and to the south the red lands of the Quadlings. All these countries have their own rulers but all four sovereigns are subject to Ozma, who is the Supreme Ruler of them all. As Pumperdink was in the north central part of the Gilliken Country, Randy realized that they must travel south to reach the Quadling Country and in that gay red Kingdom search for the castle of the Red Jinn.

It was all very exciting and mysterious, and Randy heartily hoped they would pass through the Emerald City on their way south and see the Scarecrow, the Tin Woodman and some of the other famous celebrities at Ozma's court. Perhaps they would visit the palace of Glinda, the Good Sorceress of the South and ruler of the Quadlings. Glinda would surely know something of the Red Jinn. The very sound of a Red Jinn fascinated Randy, and just as he was picturing to himself how a Jinn might look, Kabumpo

66

gave a little extra spurt of speed that carried them entirely out of the dismal forest. For a moment the sunshine made them both blink, but as they grew more accustomed to the brightness they saw that they were still in the land of the Gillikens. The fields were tinged with purple, purple flags and violets clustered around the roots of the trees and grape arbors and plum orchards were everywhere.

Panting a little from his tiring run, Kabumpo moved along more slowly, looking to the right and left for familiar landmarks. There were no towns or villages in sight, but on the other side of a small hill three roads branched off in different directions.

"Now, which road?" pondered the Elegant Elephant, swaying uncertainly from side to side. "Which road would be best?" As he did not have his specs and as the signs were too low for him to read anyway, he snatched the first sign out by the roots and held it up for Randy to read.

"This way to the river," read Randy promptly. Throwing down the first sign Kabumpo stepped over to the next road and jerked up the second.

"That way to the river," read Randy in some surprise, and when Kabumpo had torn up the third sign they both felt rather provoked.

"The other way to the river," stated the third sign contrarily.

"Well, who wants to go to the river?" grumbled the Elegant Elephant discontentedly. "Still," he flapped his ears thoughtfully, "rivers usually go some

place and it will be something to drink and wash in."

"Yes," agreed Randy not very enthusiastically, "but which way shall we go, Kabumpo, this way, that way, or the other way?" Kabumpo squinted uncertainly at the three roads. Then, as they all went in a more or less southerly direction, he tossed up Randy's sword to decide the matter.

"Point for 'this way,' hilt for 'that way,' and blade for 'the other'," announced Kabumpo, flinging the jeweled weapon high into the air. The sword embedded itself point down in the exact center of "this way"; so, restoring it to Randy, the Elegant Elephant started cautiously down the first road. There was nothing remarkable about "this way," but after the dark, tangled forest, it seemed very pleasant and interesting to the two travelers. Talking of one thing and another, but mostly of the unexpected happenings in Pumperdink, they proceeded comfortably enough, Randy standing up now and then to pluck a plum from the trees that lined the roadway, or to look for signs of a castle or cottage where they might stop for lunch. About noon they came to a sign large enough for even Kabumpo to read. "RIVER ROAD" said the sign in splashy purple letters.

"Pshaw! We knew that already," sniffed Kabumpo. "And it's about time we got to this river, if you ask me."

Randy said nothing, but looking out over Kabumpo's ears he noticed that the road had widened considerably. It seemed to the Gilliken boy that the road bed was moving and churning about, but thinking it was the reflection of the sun on the gleaming purple sands, he said nothing, and with a weary sigh Kabumpo resignedly pushed forward. But scarcely had he gone six steps before he had sunk to his shoulders in the River Road and next instant the road in a great wave rose and rolled completely over them. Gasping and choking Randy clutched Kabumpo's jeweled collar. As he did so Kabumpo got his head up.

"The river!" coughed the Elegant Elephant, wrathfully spurting out the barrel of water he had swallowed. "Not a road at all! It's a *river* road." And so it was, a tumbling rushing torrent of purple water that swept the great elephant along as if he had been a match stick. No matter how hard he tried to swim toward the shore he was immediately carried out into the center and about all he could do was to keep his own head and Randy's above water. Every time Kabumpo tried to talk, gallons of river rushed down his throat, so he finally gave up the attempt. He had already swallowed several small fish and when he thought what the river was doing to his robes and what a figure he would cut when he got out, he groaned with dismay and wretchedness.

"Oh, why didn't we go 'that way'—or 'the other way'—any way but 'this way'?" choked the poor elephant, struggling grimly with the treacherous current that rolled him about like a log. Randy, as wet and miserable as Kabumpo, hung on desperately,

bracing himself against the frequent duckings and wondering how much more he could stand. Just as he had decided things were as bad as they could possibly be, they grew terribly worse. Warned by a thunderous roar that there were rapids ahead, but unable to stop or help themselves, Randy and Kabumpo went hurling over a tremendous waterfall, down, down, down, till there actually seemed no end to the drop. How the boy kept his hold on Kabumpo's collar I cannot imagine, nor could he have told you himself, but when, bruised, battered and half drowning, he opened his eyes, he and the Elegant Elephant were still together. Kabumpo, puffing and blowing like a porpoise, was desperately fighting the treacherous river.

But now it was a fight in the dark, for the river had plunged underground and was carrying them through hollow and echoing caverns of rock and crystal. If you have ever been in a scenic railway and shot suddenly into its black, cavernous recesses, you can, in a small way, imagine how Randy felt. Only you would have to multiply that feeling by a thousand, for while scenic railways are sure to end, the Elegant Elephant and his drenched little rider had no idea at all where the underground river was taking them, or whether they would ever see daylight again. Indeed, they were so breathless and shaken by their tumble down the waterfall that they hardly noticed that the current had grown calmer, and Kabumpo rolled along for almost a mile before he realized that with a little effort he could easily reach the shore.

Then, too, as their eyes grew more accustomed to the dim darkness of the under-earth, they could see that it was not absolutely black, but a misty grey. Overhead pointed stalactites of crystal and basalt thrust their dangerous spikes downward. Each side of the river was lined with the same sharp crystal rocks. Kabumpo, splashing toward the right bank, looked worriedly for a place where he could land without puncturing himself. At last he sighted a stretch of smooth black rock almost level with the river and with a huge grunt hoisted himself up and out of the mischievous stream.

"Something to drink and wash in," shuddered Kabumpo, giving himself a cautious shake so as not to unseat Randy. "I was never so sick of water, inside and out, in my life. I feel like a sponge and an aquarium. Br—rah! A fine place this is! We might just as well have disappeared with the King. Br—rah!"

"I'm c-c-cold," shivered Randy, sliding down Kabumpo's trunk and trying to squeeze the water out of his clothes.

"Me too!" grunted the Elegant Elephant, trying

WITH A HUGE GRUNT KABUMPO HOISTED HIMSELF OUT

to beat himself in the chest with his trunk, "and if my tusks weren't so far apart they'd chatter, and I'm hungry enough to eat monkey meat."

"Elephants don't eat meat." Randy had to grin at Kabumpo's savage expression.

"No, they don't eat meat and they hate monkeys, but I'm so starved that if I saw a monkey, I'd eat it like that!" Snapping his trunk, Kabumpo began to run around in a circle, with Randy right behind him.

After the tenth round they felt a little better and began to examine the strange cavern. The rock on which they had landed was the only safe place for Kabumpo to tread, for as far as they could see in both directions the river was edged with the sharp and needle-pointed crystals. At the back of the rock a sheer wall of metal rose to the top of the long, dim passageway. Tiptoeing over to this wall, Randy gave it an experimental tap with his knuckles and found to his surprise that the wall was quite hot. He called Kabumpo and they both pressed against it as hard as they could in an endeavor to get warm and dry. In fact, the Elegant Elephant pressed so hard that the wall, with a great grind and creak, swayed inward, and before you could say Ozmo-

75

potamus Randy and Kabumpo tumbled over on the other side.

It must have been a door!" exclaimed Randy, jumping up as fast as he could. Kabumpo was lying

on his back, his four feet sticking up in the air, grunting and sputtering with disgust.

"Doornation!" raged the Elegant Elephant, lurching to his feet. As he did so, the metal door swung back into place and they found themselves shut up

76

in a huge, iron-walled chamber. In the center of the rock floor a fire fountain threw sprays of sparks into the air and to the two cold and shivering adventurers the warmth seemed perfectly delicious.

"Wherever do you suppose we are, Kabumpo?" whispered Randy, looking fearfully around the great, grim, empty room.

"Ask me again in five minutes," wheezed the Elegant Elephant, making for the fire fountain with long energetic strides. I'm going to get warm and dry. Then maybe I can think of something. At any rate, it's better in here than outside."

Randy wasn't so sure, but following Kabumpo's example he began drying himself at the fire fountain. They were both so busy turning round and round that neither noticed the opening of fifty round doors in the iron wall. And next instant, with a roar that sounded like the explosion of fifty guns, the inhabitants of the cavern hurled themselves at the intruders. Snatching Randy up in his trunk, Kabumpo, trembling in every leg, saw fifty projectiles shaped like torpedoes coming straight at them.

Turning sideways and holding Randy so as to protect him by his own huge body Kabumpo shuddered and closed his eyes. He could almost feel the

77

horrid missiles piercing his elegant hide. This, then, was the end. Who now would rescue the royal family of Pumperdink or save the unhappy kingdom from the misrule of Faleero and Kettywig? This and a hundred other gloomy thoughts flashed through the Elegant Elephant's mind as he awaited destruction. He was astonished at the time it was taking the torpedoes to reach and riddle him. Finally, unable to bear the suspense any longer, he opened one eye and glanced wildly over his shoulder.

CHAPTER 6

Torpedora, the Glorious

IN a neat and precise row, fifty torpedoes stood upright before him. Not merely torpedoes, but torpedomen and women. They had strong, smooth iron-clad bodies with no legs or feet, but their fire arms were held close to their cylindrical sides, and their heads ended in sharp, dangerous-looking points. Their black and shining faces were neither cruel nor ferocious, and taking heart, Kabumpo set Randy

have just left the furnace. These he sulkily offered to the visitors, and when Kabumpo and the boy jumped away from him in real alarm, he dropped the basket on the floor and began shooting round and round examining the two from every angle.

"Pray eat!" directed the Queen, graciously extending her fire arms. "You will find our doughnuts very strengthening." Randy looked desperately at the Elegant Elephant, but Kabumpo seemed equal to any emergency.

"We only eat at night, your Highness," murmured Kabumpo apologetically. "If we were to partake of food in the daytime we would be utterly destroyed. It is the way we are made," he finished, with a sly look at Randy. The Queen seemed unconvinced, but without giving her time to argue the matter, Kabumpo plunged into a lively account of their adventures. He had just got to the disappearance of the royal family, when Torpedora interrupted him with an imperious gesture.

"Stop!" cried her Majesty in a threatening voice. "Where is this Pumperdink? Have you ever heard of such a kingdom, Dodo?"

"No, no! Absolutely no, no!" screeched the Dodo, in a raucous croak. "There is no such place, your

Highness!" Settling himself in an iron swing just above the Queen's head, he began to swing himself vigorously back and forth, emitting such villainous screams and screeches that Kabumpo could not make himself heard at all.

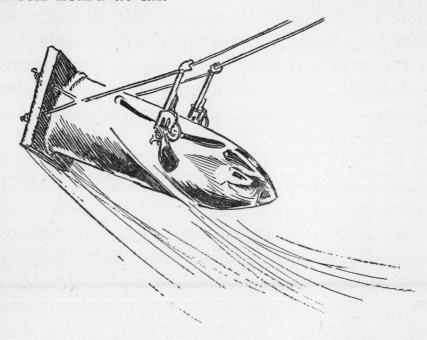

"Just leave out Pumperdink and go on from there," sniffed the Queen, as Dodo finally left off screeching.

"If I leave out Pumperdink there's no use going on at all," snapped Kabumpo, who had been rumbling like a volcano during Dodo's ear-splitting racket.

83

"Then why go on?" inquired Torpedora, showing a double row of small black teeth as she smiled sweetly at Kabumpo. "Stories make me so very tired and sleepy, especially stories that are not true. Ah, I have it!" The Queen clapped her hands gleefully. "I'll keep you for riddles. Every day we will guess who you are and how you came here. It ought to last for days and days and then—" her Majesty gave Kabumpo a second dazzling smile "—and then we'll riddle you through and through and sweep you into the fire fountain."

"Well, won't that be nice?" Randy edged closer to Kabumpo and looked with positive aversion at the iron Queen.

"It's no use talking to these idiots," snorted the Elegant Elephant temperishly. "I shan't open my mouth again." He gave a furious sniff, however, as the Queen, with a stiff little bow, excused herself.

"It's high time I was torpedozing," yawned her Highness in a bored voice, and signaling wearily to her subjects she shot majestically into the air. Followed by the whole fifty and Torpedodo, she circled around the iron chamber and then with fifty-one little clicks they disappeared into the small metal compartments in the wall.

"Well, what," gulped the Elegant Elephant, sitting down with a thump, "what do you think of that? Never have I been treated with such cast-iron impertinence, never—in my whole elephant life."

"We'd better go while they are asleep," breathed

Randy, running over to the great metal door.

"Yes, while they are torpedozing we'll leave!" agreed Kabumpo, hot-footing it quickly after Randy. "If we stay here we'll be riddled, and a nice thing that would be."

"And I used to like riddles," sighed Randy pensively. "But liking riddles and being riddled are not the same thing at all. How do you open this door, anyway?"

"Another riddle," panted Kabumpo, hurling himself at the heavy structure. But push and thump as he would the door refused to budge. As he paused to rest and mop his forehead, Torpedodo whizzed suddenly from his hole in the wall.

"That door only opens once in every hundred years," jeered Dodo vindictively. "Ha, ha! You'll have to wait a while!" And returning like a flash to his iron aperture he went in and slammed the door, leaving Kabumpo and Randy too discouraged and exhausted even to speak. The air, which had seemed pleasantly warm when they were wet and shivering, was now so hot and crackling that they could hardly breathe and the terrible heat, added to their hunger, made it imperative for them to escape as soon as possible.

"I can't stand—much—more—of—this!" panted Kabumpo, flapping his ears unhappily. "And say, I'd give my best suspenders for just one peanut."

"Maybe there's another door," suggested Randy, but before they had gone halfway around the great room a storm came up, or rather down, and they were a hundred times more uncomfortable than before. Each rain drop was a torpedo that exploded spitefully when it struck the ground. After three had set fire to Randy's hair and another had burned a hole in his coat, Kabumpo made the boy lie down and then stood carefully over him. Thus Randy was protected but the poor elephant was peppered with the stinging missiles and had to blow and beat himself constantly with his trunk to put out the tiny fires that the torpedoes started in his cloak. And when at last the storm abated his velvet robe was little more than a blackened mass of holes held together by tiny threads of silk.

"Oh, well," sighed Kabumpo resignedly, as Randy rolled out and looked at him in shocked silence, "I've always wanted a smoking jacket and now I've got one."

Randy jumped to his feet and gave the big elephant a quick hug. "Kabumpo," marvelled the boy softly, "you're grand! I don't see how you can joke when you're all singed and scorched and we're both liable to be riddled."

"Humph!" sniffed Kabumpo grimly. "I'm too old to cry, so I may as well laugh. Now for that door.

87

EACH RAINDROP WAS A TORPEDO THAT EXPLODED SPITEFULLY

Ha!" Rubbing the cinders from his eyes, the Elegant Elephant marched determinedly along the north wall, feeling every inch of the way with his trunk. In the very center he came to a small iron ring.

"This may set off an alarm or blow us to bits," grumbled the Elegant Elephant, "but anything's better than this."

"Let me pull it," begged Randy, who wished to take his share of the danger and felt that so far Kabumpo had borne the brunt of their hardships. "Let me pull it." And before Kabumpo could interfere he gave the iron ring a furious tug. A loud bell sounded in the west wall and as the two prisoners anxiously waited for something to happen, Dodo burst from his cell again and hurled himself downward.

"What do you want? Who told you to ring my bell? Don't you know I must obey the bell ringer, no matter who he is?"

"Oh, Kabumpo, did you hear that?" squealed Randy, beginning to hop up and down with excitement.

Kabumpo certainly had.

"Show us the way out of here," he trumpeted fiercely. "Quick, before I wring your iron neck."

Dodo gave a frightened squeak at this terrible threat, and motioning for them to follow flew straight to the north wall and tapped twice on the panel with his fire claw. Without a sound it slid aside and without stopping to thank the rude creature or say good-bye

to Torpedo Town, Kabumpo rushed through the opening.

"Be careful," warned Randy, who was riding perilously between the Elegant Elephant's ears. "Remember the river!"

"I'd like to drink a gallon of river right now," puffed Kabumpo, fairly panting with thirst and exhaustion. "Why, I'd even jump in it."

But there was no river on the other side of Torpedo Town, only a long, dim tunnel that seemed to slant gradually upward. But the air was cool and with a profound sigh of relief, Kabumpo began to climb the slight incline. They had gone possibly half a mile when they came to a turn in the tunnel and found themselves facing an immense grey curtain. It billowed in and out and they could distinctly hear voices and footsteps on the other side. On the curtain itself, after some difficulty, they made out ten words.

THIS IS STAIR WAY.
STEP UP AND STATE YOUR BUSINESS.

"Well, that's fair enough," mumbled Kabumpo, after squinting thoughtfully at these instructions. So, parting the curtains with his trunk, he called in a loud voice:

"Way for the Elegant Elephant of Oz and Randy, the Gilliken, who seek the castle of the Red Jinn! Way for the Elegant Elephant of Oz!" Then, forgetting to step up, he fell forward on his knees, throwing Randy over his head.

91

CHAPTER 7

Stair Way

THERE was a short silence as Randy and Kabumpo fell through the curtain. Randy, the first
to regain his feet, saw an immense flight of irregular
steps straggling upward. Each step was as low and
flat and broad as a city street. Crooked little stone
houses were built on the edges of each step and
a line of crooked and stooped people with eyes as
large as plums turned to stare at the travelers. As

Kabumpo and Randy stood uncertainly at the bottom of Stair Way a hoarse voice came booming down to them:

"Welcome to Stair Way! Come up! Keep moving! Look where you're going! Go where you're looking!"

"It's the King," fluttered a little Stare on the lowest tread. "Come, my stepchildren. Come to your stepmother. Keep moving, keep moving. Do as his Majesty commands." At this, all the Stares, who had stopped to gaze at the newcomers, began to move upward, but over their shoulders they stared without winking at Kabumpo and Randy. It made the boy feel positively creepy, but the Elegant Elephant, with an indifferent shrug, cautiously started up the crowded steps.

"We have to go up anyway," muttered Kabumpo, to show that it was not the King's orders that influenced him. "Have you no children of your own, madam?" he inquired loftily of the crooked little Stare Lady who was anxiously shepherding a stoop-shouldered boy and girl out of his path.

"We're all step-relations here," explained the little woman, rolling her huge purple eyes around at Kabumpo. "Stepmothers, stepfathers, stepsisters, stepbrothers, stepchildren, step—"

"Step lively," shouted the King's voice again from the top of the stair, and old and young, little and big, began to crowd and push in an endeavor to reach the top.

"It's a shame!" breathed Randy indignantly. "Must you keep doing this all the time?"

"What else is there to do?" asked the little step-mother who had first addressed them. "What else could one do in Stair Way but go up and down? That's why we're here, to step and stare, to stare and step. It's beautiful!" she finished earnestly.

"Step by step one goes a long way," said Kabumpo under his breath. "Ha, ha! But not for me."

"We look you up, we look you down,
    For that is the rule in our beautiful town;
    And first we walk up and then we walk down,
    And keep moving all day; it's the way in our town!"

chanted the Stares, opening their eyes still wider and wider.

"How perfectly awful!" yawned Kabumpo, who was by this time so tired and hungry he could hardly keep his feet. "Well, why do you have houses if you keep moving up and down this way?"

"Oh, just to step in and out of," beamed the step-mother. "What do other people do with houses?"

"Not much more than that, nowadays," admitted the Elegant Elephant. "Say, are we almost at the top?"

"Do you not see the castles?" exclaimed a step-uncle, raising his arm importantly. Randy, holding

on to Kabumpo's ear, stood up to have a look, but all he discovered were two enormous stepladders, one on each side of the top step of Stair Way Town. A bent and crooked King with a scepter that looked like a banister rail was scurrying up one ladder and a

95

stooped and savage-looking Queen was backing awkwardly down the other.

"King Kumup and Queen Godown," whispered the little stepmother, who was walking sedately beside Kabumpo.

"And do they really run up and down those ladders all day?" gasped Randy, watching the two sovereigns intently.

"Been doing it for years," boasted the step-uncle who was on the other side of the Elegant Elephant. But he had time for no more, for just then Kabumpo reached the top step and the Queen, jumping off her ladder and flashing her great purple eyes in a royal and dangerous fashion, bawled imperiously:

"Go down!" With frightened little bows the Stares turned and started obediently downward.

"Go down!" shouted her Majesty, again pointing a furious finger at Kabumpo. "I said GO DOWN!"

"I heard you," observed the Elegant Elephant, calmly regarding the crooked little Queen, "but, unfortunately, I have other plans." Kabumpo swung his trunk unconcernedly.

"Other plans!" raged the Queen, opening her purple eyes so wide that Randy thought they would roll down her cheeks, while the King, who had reached

the top of the ladder, brandished his scepter men-
acingly.

"It's against the law to stop on the stairs," roared
the King indignantly. "Move on! Move on, or we'll

take steps against you. Whoever stops on the stair
is liable to be kicked down the whole flight!"

"Now I shouldn't try that," advised Kabumpo, with
an amused wink around at Randy. Then, as the
Queen actually gave him a feeble push and the King

in his anger and excitement fell all the way down the ladder and landed on his head, the Elegant Elephant dodged between the sputtering sovereigns and plunged through the grey curtains just behind the step-castles.

"Im—agine spending your life on the stairs," exclaimed Randy, looking curiously over his shoulder. But Kabumpo had neither the time nor the inclination to look back. Hurrying along the earthy passageway in which he now found himself he looked eagerly ahead for some signs of an outlet that would take them back to upper and outer Oz.

"I never cared for these underground peoples and places," sniffed Kabumpo, pounding determinedly along the empty passageway. "I hope to goodness we've not gone too far out of our way. Looks like a mine," he decided, not very enthusiastically.

"Well, I wonder whose mine it is," called Randy, trying to see around the corner of the long corridor.

"Mine!" laughed a silvery voice, and down from a ledge just above their heads floated a little grey elfin lady wearing a filigreed silver crown on her long silver hair, a spun silver dress, and tiny silver slippers.

"Well, I'm certainly glad it is yours," said Kabumpo, glancing thoughtfully down at the pretty little creature. "Are you an elf or a fairy, my dear?"

"My name is Delva!" answered the small silver lady, looking fearlessly up at the huge elephant. "I am Queen of the Delves and this is my silver mine. Will you stay here and help us delve, dig, and bore for silver?"

"Not if we can help it," muttered Kabumpo under his breath. But Delva, without waiting for his consent, clapped her small hands sharply. Instantly the passageway swarmed with delves. On their heads they wore silver helmets with long pointed spikes and on their hands, like gauntlets, they had spiked silver claws. As Randy stared doubtfully at these strange little men, Delva stamped her foot and immediately the whole band hurled themselves at the walls of the tunnel, burrowing with their heads and scratching with their claws till they had vanished like so many moles.

"You see how easy it is," smiled Delva, powdering her nose energetically with a small box of silver powder. "Just come with me and I'll have our silversmith fit you out with gloves and helmets."

"But we can't stay here," began Randy, as Delva skipped gaily ahead of Kabumpo. "We're saving a

King and Queen and we have to find the Red Jinn, don't we Kabumpo?"

"Yes," said the Elegant Elephant stiffly. "Besides, mining would bore us to death."

"Bore you to death!" Delva stopped short and

tapped her silver slipper angrily on the silver-flagged flooring. "Why, that's an idea! That's just what I'll do. You refuse to work? Very well, then, you shall be bored to death by my army of Delves."

Raising a silver whistle to her lips, and looking not nearly so pretty as she had looked before, Delva blew three shrill blasts. But Kabumpo was weary of the strange manners and behavior of these underground rulers and without waiting for the whistle to take effect, he seized Delva in his trunk, set her unceremoniously on a high rock above his head and went thumping like an express train down the winding corridor of the silver mine. Soon they heard hundreds of tiny footsteps pattering behind them and as Kabumpo came to the end of the corridor and plunged headlong into the small room at the end, the first of the Silver Queen's army came shouting into view. Slamming the door of the tiny compartment, which was quite dark and stifling, Kabumpo felt angrily around for a stick or some other weapon, but Randy gave a startled scream.

"We're moving!" cried Randy delightedly. "Oh, Kabumpo—it's an elevator and you must have started it when you shut the door."

"Good luck at last," panted Kabumpo, as they shot dizzily upward. "And about time, too." And it really was good luck this time, for when the elevator did stop and they cautiously opened the door, they found themselves on top of the world again looking out over the pleasant fields, valleys and woods of the Gillikens. And better still, over the tree tops just ahead rose the turrets and spires of an imposing castle. The sun was sinking behind the purple hills, the birds were twittering happily in the lacy branches of the tulip trees and never had the sky seemed more bright or beautiful. Stepping from the elevator, which at once shot down to the bottom of the shaft, Kabumpo started on a run for the castle.

"Hah, now we shall soon be with people who understand and appreciate us," puffed the Elegant Elephant thankfully, "people of our own rank and station!"

Forgetting that Randy was only a poor mountain boy, and that he himself in his scorched and tattered cloak presented anything but a royal appearance, Kabumpo rushed confidently through the castle garden and thumped loudly on the castle door.

"Wait!" whispered Randy, his teeth beginning to chatter a little from fright and weariness. "There's something very odd about this castle. Have you noticed the size of the door, and look, all the windows are at the top." As Kabumpo drew back to see for himself, the door, which was in truth thirty feet high and thirty feet across, slowly creaked open and

102

a giant stood looking curiously down at them. Randy was too stunned to speak and Kabumpo too weary to run and as they stood silently regarding him, the giant burst into a hearty roar.

"Welcome! Welcome!" Leaning down he shook Kabumpo's trunk as if it had been a pump handle. "Welcome to the Castle of Nandywog, and you are just in time for dinner, too."

"Whose?" asked Randy in a faint voice, for he had read some extremely disturbing facts about giants.

"Why, MINE!" beamed the giant gaily, and leaning over he picked up Kabumpo as if he had been a toy dog and carried him boisterously into the castle.

CHAPTER 8

Nandywog, the Little Giant

K ABUMPO had never felt so small and insignificant in his whole life and when the giant set him on the floor his legs wobbled so strangely that he had to lean against a three-legged stool for support.

"Oh," shivered the boy anxiously to himself. "Oh —I hope I am going to be brave!" Grasping his jeweled sword firmly by the handle he waited desperately for the giant's next move. But Nandywog, now that they were inside his castle, seemed perfectly satisfied, and stretching himself full length upon the floor so he could better observe his small visitors, he regarded them long and seriously.

"Was it a fire or an explosion?" he asked finally, fixing his great eyes curiously on Kabumpo's scorched and tattered cloak.

"A little of both," admitted Kabumpo in a relieved voice, for the giant's question was so frank and friendly that it filled the Elegant Elephant with new hope and confidence. "We fell in a river, were carried underground to Torpedo Town, got caught in a torpedo storm, escaped through Stair Way and a silver mine and coming to your castle hoped we might obtain rest and refreshment before continuing our journey."

"And so you shall! So you shall!" promised Nandywog heartily. "I can see you are both brave and interesting. You neither run nor scream when you see a giant. You are the only people in all Oz who have treated me as a fellow being. Even my own subjects jump like rabbits when I approach. Nobody will talk to me, or visit me. I believe I am the loneliest person in this whole country." Nandywog sighed

105

gustily and rolling over on his back stared up at the ceiling. "Being a giant is awful—awful! Especially when you are a little giant," he finished gloomily.

"Oh—are you a little giant?" asked Randy in surprise, for Nandywog seemed simply enormous to him.

"The littlest giant in Oz," answered Nandy. "When I grew no taller than twenty feet, my own people flung me off Big Top Mountain. The giants will have nothing to do with me because I am too small and the Ozites will have nothing to do with me because I am too big. Terrible, isn't it?"

Kabumpo thought it best to agree and shook his head sympathetically. "So," continued Nandywog mournfully, "I traveled all over Oz till I came to this valley and the Tripedalians were so frightened they did everything I told them to do. So I told them to build me this castle and they did, and now they bring me everything I need or ask for, but although I am as kind and considerate as I can be they are still afraid and my life is hard and lonely.

"And who are these Tripedalians?" inquired Kabumpo, hoping the giant would soon stop talking and offer them something to eat. "I never even heard of them." Nandywog, instead of answering, leaned over and pulled the bell rope beside the door. So quickly that it made Randy jump, a fat little servitor appeared in the doorway. He was about the same size as the boy himself but there the similarity ceased, for the giant's servant was round and ruddy and his plump body was supported by three sturdy

legs and feet. He kept hopping from one foot to the other in a way that made Randy exceedingly uneasy.

"Did you ring, sir?" he quavered in a scared voice.

"Certainly," rumbled the giant gruffly. "Can't you see we have visitors? Serve the dinner at once, Kojo.

Er—er—what would you like to have?" he inquired, turning his head toward the Elegant Elephant.

"Oh, just bring me a hundred pounds of hay, ten quarts of crushed vegetables, ten quarts of oats and barley and a barrel of peanuts," ordered Kabumpo calmly. Kojo's mouth fell open, but the giant seemed to find nothing strange about the elephant's dinner.

"How about the boy?" he asked politely.

"Oh, I'll take whatever you have," decided Randy quickly, and Kojo, after an indignant glance at Kabumpo, went hippety-hopping out of the room.

"Do they all have three legs?" asked Randy, sliding down Kabumpo's trunk and seating himself comfortably on the floor beside Nandywog, or rather beside Nandywog's nose. The giant nodded and smiled kindly at the boy.

"Tri-pedals, three feet," he explained gravely. Every one has three legs and feet, excepting me— the cows, the mice and even the chickens!"

"Why, so have the tables and chairs!" exclaimed Randy in astonishment. And this was perfectly true. Every chair, table, chest, stand and stool had three legs and as Kabumpo and Nandywog began conversing learnedly about the three-legged inhabitants of the valley, Randy stepped around the giant's hall examining everything with lively interest and curiosity. The windows high above his head were set at just the proper height for Nandywog and all the furnishings were giant size, too. But small doors had been cut in the large doors for the giant's servants and slanting runways led up to the tables, side boards, cupboards and book shelves.

It was fun to watch the Tripedalians setting the table, bustling importantly up the broad runway with the giant's huge knives, forks, spoons and tremendous saucers and plates. They put a small table and chair for Randy upon the giant's table itself and piled Kabumpo's hay, vegetables and peanuts in a great flat flower dish in the center. Then Kojo, who seemed to be in charge, climbed a ladder and struck the huge dinner gong hanging on the wall.

Chuckling and rubbing his hands together, Nandywog invited his guests into the dining hall. Kabumpo he lifted ceremoniously to the center of the table, but Randy, not wishing to repeat the breath-taking sensation of his first lift, ran up the slanting board used by the servants and cheerfully seated himself at the small table beside the giant's tumbler. There, with scarcely concealed eagerness, the boy waited for the feast to begin.

Three roast oxen and two roast pigs, each borne by four Tripedalians, were served first and Nandy-wog cut small slices from each for his young visitor. Then, staggering up the board with dishes as big as bath tubs, ten more Tripedalian footmen served the giant with vegetables, salad and a tasty pudding. Never had Randy been so famished and never had food tasted more delicious. The giant kept filling and refilling his plate till he could not swallow another morsel. Kabumpo, forgetting his rank and royalty, stowed away all the provisions the Tripedalians had brought him and loudly trumpeted for more hay. This made the giant laugh so heartily that he nearly blew Randy into the pudding dish and soon they were all rocking with mirth and merriment and, in spite of their difference in weight and stature, joking together like old friends at a birthday party. Even the servants hippety-hopping about began to look less scared and nervous.

"Do stay, stay a long time," begged Nandywog, beaming down at his small visitors. "Stay with me always and you shall live like kings in my castle. Why, I haven't been so happy since I was a boy on Big Top Mountain."

Kabumpo, assured by now of Nandywog's friend-

THE TRIPEDALIANS SET THE GIANT'S TABLE

111

liness, thought it time to tell him the whole cause and purpose of their journey. The little giant was tremendously interested in the curious story and promised to do all he could to help them. Tripedalia, he explained, was on the edge of the Gilliken Country

and scarcely a day's journey from the Emerald City, and going into the library the obliging fellow looked through all his maps and history books for some information concerning the Red Jinn. But he could find no reference at all to this strange wizard. Still, he, like Kabumpo, felt that his castle must be in the Quadling Country of Oz.

"Why not come with us?" asked Randy, who was walking composedly up and down the giant's shoulder. He had taken a great fancy to Nandywog. "Please do come!"

"I would only get you in trouble," sighed the giant, shaking his head sorrowfully. "Everywhere I go, people immediately take me for an enemy and though they can do me no serious harm, it is distinctly unpleasant to have a fire hose turned on one from the roof, or an army of soldiers shooting at my shins. No, here I am known and safe. Here I will stay. But when you have rescued the King and Royal Family of Pumperdink you must come back to visit me, for you are the only friends I have in all this great land of Oz."

Kabumpo was not sure he could be spared but Randy earnestly promised to return and after toasting themselves a while at the giant's fire the two begged leave to retire for the night. Randy, in a three legged bed as big as a house, slept soundly and well, while Kabumpo, who seldom lay down, dozed fitfully beside the window. The giant's housekeeper, while they rested, made Kabumpo a new

113

robe from two of Nandy's best silk handkerchiefs, so that he looked quite his old and elegant self when they made ready to depart. There seemed no end to Nandywog's thoughtfulness and after a hearty breakfast, and carrying with them a still heartier lunch, the travelers again turned their faces toward the south. It was with real regret that they said good-bye to the little giant and Nandywog stood in the door of his castle and waved and waved till they were out of sight.

Now Tripedalia is a small, three-cornered country with three-cornered cottages, three-cornered fields, parks and flower beds. The three-legged people hopping briskly about their three-legged business nodded pleasantly to Randy and Kabumpo as they passed, and to see the three-legged sheep and cows quietly grazing in the pastures made the boy laugh outright with interest and amusement.

"We'll always remember this as one of the good places, won't we Kabumpo?" Randy sighed and looked dreamily back at the giant's castle.

"We must take the good with the bad," answered the Elegant Elephant philosophically. "Traveling is that way, my boy." Kabumpo had not enjoyed the giant as thoroughly as Randy. He was used to being the biggest person present and Nandywog made him feel ridiculously small and unimportant. He was far more comfortable nodding condescendingly to the fat and amiable little Tripedalians and stepping hugely and majestically down their narrow streets

and lanes. Tripedalia was not large and in an hour they had come to the end of the pleasant valley, and waving his trunk graciously to a three-legged farmer plowing with his three-legged horse, Kabumpo stepped through the narrow pass between two hills at the valley's end.

115

"This should bring us out right on the edge of the Emerald City," predicted Randy eagerly. "Hello— but what's this?"

"A couple of dummies probably," muttered the Elegant Elephant, surveying two rotund little guardsmen who blocked the way at the other end of the pass. "Move aside there!" he called haughtily. But the guards, who seemed really to be dummies, neither moved nor spoke. If they had not rolled their eyes so drolly, Randy would have thought they were just figures set up to frighten off intruders.

"Why, they're rubber!" he gasped, after a long, curious inspection. "Just look at them, Kabumpo!" This Kabumpo proceeded to do and after a short, contemptuous sniff he again ordered the guards to move out of his way.

"Who are you, fellows?" he inquired irritably, and as neither guardsman moved nor spoke, he gave the first a sharp poke in the chest with his trunk.

"Squee!" yelled the guard, bouncing into the air with a broad grin.

"Gee!" squealed the other, as Kabumpo thumped him as hard as he had thumped his comrade. Then both rubber men bowed politely and waved their arms for the Elegant Elephant to follow them.

THE SQUEE GEES

117

"Were you squeaking to me?" puffed Kabumpo, swaying angrily from side to side. The guards nodded and snorting with indignation the Elegant Elephant thudded after them.

"They must be Squee Gees," whispered Randy. "Oh, look, it's a revolution! Or a war!" Following the guards, Kabumpo had walked directly into the public square of a comical Rubber City. Rubber blocks paved the streets so that the Elegant Elephant bounced high into the air at every step. Rubber trees lined the avenues and rubber houses in neat rows faced the visitors. Birds, shaped like barnyard hens, bounced from tree to tree whistling every time they struck against a branch.

"Fowl ball!" grunted Kabumpo, as one of the birds hit him between the eyes, and not wishing to bounce about himself, he stopped perfectly still and waited to see what would happen. All the inhabitants were bouncing wildly by this time. Not only that, they were thumping each other vigorously in the chest, at each punch emitting sharp, excited cries and speeches.

Almost deafened by the uproar but feeling terribly amused nevertheless, Randy, like Kabumpo, waited curiously for the Squee Gees to address them.

CHAPTER 9

The Guide Post Man

"WHY, they're just like Pajonia's rubber dolls," muttered Kabumpo at last. He had been watching the Squee Gees very closely for several minutes. "They can't squeak unless you squeeze them. Look! To speak they have to punch each other. It's not a battle at all, just a conversation. They are talking about us. Ho! Ha! Kerumph! And they don't like us at all. How far is this city from

119

the capital of Oz?" trumpeted Kabumpo, snatching a Squee Gee baker up in his trunk.

"Three hundred bounds and two bounces," squeaked the baker, one word to each hug the Elegant Elephant gave him. "Exqueeze me, please."

"Certainly!" roared Kabumpo, dropping the baker so hard that he bounced over a rubber tree. "I vote we go," he added in an undertone to Randy. "In a minute they'll start punching us and then there'll be a regular game of ball."

"I'd like to have something to remind me of the place," said Randy, who could scarcely take his eyes off the bouncing, bounding, boisterous Squee Gees.

"All right, but be quick about it," advised Kabumpo. "How about some of those rubber flowers?"

"Just what I was thinking." Sliding to the ground, Randy seized a rubber rose in both hands. The stem, instead of breaking, stretched and stretched, and as the boy gave it an especially hard tug it snapped off and gave him a stinging blow on the nose. His action seemed to infuriate the Squee Gees. Bouncing up to him they began squeezing and thumping him on the chest till he was positively breathless. Kabumpo could not help laughing when the rose hit Randy, but seeing that matters were now really serious, he pushed the rubber men right and left and lifting Randy in his trunk charged headfirst through the crowd. Each time Kabumpo touched the rubber paving blocks he went twenty feet upward and twenty feet forward so that in less than ten springs and a

bounce he was entirely out of bounds and out of Squee Gee Ville. Indeed, the last bounce carried them over the city wall and landed them, terribly tossed about and breathless, in the middle of a hay field.

121

"Grapes and grandywogs!" exploded Kabumpo crossly, feeling himself all over with his trunk. "For two straws I'd go back and puncture the whole population. Why didn't we think of that before? Well, here's lunch, anyway, and high time for it, too." Randy's nose was still red and swollen, but he could not help grinning as the Elegant Elephant made savage lunges at a huge stack of hay. He himself had a big box of sandwiches the giant had ordered put up for him and unstrapping the box from his shoulders he too began to eat, thinking as he did so of all the curious experiences he had had since leaving Pumperdink.

"I wonder if that soothsayer told the truth," he observed presently. "Do you suppose this Red Jinn can really restore the King and the others?"

"I really do!" answered the Elegant Elephant with conviction. "And instead of wasting time at the capital telling our story to Ozma and the Wizard of Oz, we'll just skirt the Emerald City and push right on to the Quadling country. Have you noticed anything special about this field of hay, my boy?" Randy nodded, for his mouth was full of chicken. Then with a hasty swallow he waved toward the fences.

"Green!" he cried triumphantly. "So we are out of

the Gilliken country and the Quadling country must be somewhere just below. I wish I could see Ozma and the Scarecrow and the Cowardly Lion," he added, a bit wistfully.

"Plenty of time for that when we've saved Pumperdink," answered Kabumpo sternly. "After we have rescued Pompus and his family, you and I will travel all over Oz," he promised grandly. "Nothing to keep us home, you know."

Randy smiled a little at this, but saying nothing he straightened the Elegant Elephant's robe and settled himself cozily in back of Kabumpo's left ear.

"Suppose the Red Jinn does not live in the Quadling country after all," he said quietly, as Kabumpo started diagonally across the hay field.

"What are you trying to do? Spoil my lunch?" Flapping his huge ears like sails, Kabumpo quickened his pace and brushing aside the green fence with one push of his trunk swung confidently out on a broad and prosperous looking highway. In the distance they could see the gleaming turrets of Ozma's castle and Randy could not help thinking it would save them both time and trouble to stop and ask Ozma the exact location of the Red Jinn's palace. But Kabumpo, without turning his head once

123

in the direction of the Emerald City, hustled down the highway and in an hour they passed under the crimson arch leading into the Red Lands of Oz.

"Well, here we are!" announced the Elegant Elephant cheerfully. "Here we are!" The arch stood on the crest of a hill, and spreading invitingly out before them were the red plains and valleys, the small towns and stately castles of the Quadlings.

"This Jinn may live in any one of those castles!" exclaimed Kabumpo, waving his trunk impressively from left to right. There were five castles in plain view and very much excited and encouraged he started down the hill. A narrow footpath led through a small red wood at the bottom and anxious to reach the first castle as soon as possible the Elegant Elephant broke into a run. Emerging from the wood he almost collided with a sturdy guide post standing at a fork in the roads.

"What does it say?" asked Randy, as Kabumpo, grumbling a little, backed off.

"Never heard a guide post say anything and this one doesn't even point," answered Kabumpo impatiently. "What good is it anyway?"

"Why, it has a face painted on its knob," cried Randy. "Maybe the directions are on the back."

Chapter Nine

Walking stiffly around the post the Elegant Elephant pricked up his ears at what he saw.

THIS GUIDE POST MAN WILL DIRECT OR TAKE YOU ANYWHERE, stated a small sign on the Post Man's back.

"Is he alive?" Sliding quickly to the ground Randy squinted up at the jolly looking Post Man. "Great Gillikens, did you see that wink?" Kabumpo certainly did and as it did not seem at all respectful for a wooden post to wink at an Elegant Elephant, Kabumpo shook his trunk severely.

"Kindly direct us to the castle of the Red Jinn," he ordered haughtily. At this the Post Man merely closed one painted eye and yawned terrifically.

"Maybe he's deaf," volunteered Randy, as the Guide Post Man opened his eye and looked thoughtfully off into space. "Why, of course he's deaf! Deaf as a post. He *is* a post, you know."

"He's a fraud!" raged Kabumpo, lurching forward angrily. "What does he mean, standing there like a stick and yawning in my face and not lifting a finger to help us?"

"Wait!" begged Randy, as Kabumpo raised his trunk threateningly. "There may be some more directions. Oh, there are!"

125

Walking sulkily after Randy, Kabumpo saw a small box like a letter box attached to the Post Man's back.

POST ENQUIRIES HERE, directed a notice on the box. "Got a pencil?" Feeling in his own pocket, Randy

found one himself before Kabumpo had time to look, and tearing a sheet from a small memorandum book he scribbled hastily: "Where is the castle of the Red Jinn?" Dropping the paper in the box Randy and Kabumpo hurried to the other side and stared expectantly into the Post Man's face. What happened was quite upsetting, especially to Randy. The Guide Post Man's two wooden arms, which had been tightly pressed to his sides, now flew up violently. One knocked Randy over like a ten pin and the other hit Kabumpo a fearful blow on the trunk.

"Oh—ouch!" roared the Elegant Elephant, stamping one foot and then the other. "Such manners! If I were the King of this country I'd chop off your knob and burn you for firewood. I'd tear you down and root you up and smash you into splinters!"

"What's the use of shouting like that when he can't even hear you?" Rubbing his head, Randy picked himself up and looked rather angrily at the Post Man himself.

"Why, he's trying to point the way to the Jinn's castle. We were too close to him, that's all!" he exclaimed suddenly. "See, he has both arms pointed northwest!"

"But we just came from the north," answered Kabumpo, with an exasperated snort. "Didn't I tell you the Red Jinn's castle was in the south?"

"Yes, but that doesn't make it in the south," persisted Randy calmly. "It may not be in Oz at all!"

"Not in Oz at all! Great Grump, are you crazy?

127

Have we come all this distance to take our orders from a stupid blockhead like this? Pay no attention to the wooden pest. Come on, he has wasted enough of our time already." Glaring at the Post Man, who winked first one eye and then the other, Kabumpo turned on his heel and began moving slowly down the road. But Randy was not so sure the Post Man was wrong. Walking quickly around he carefully reread the sign on the fellow's back: THIS GUIDE POST MAN WILL DIRECT OR TAKE YOU ANYWHERE.

"I wonder if he really would," pondered the boy thoughtfully, and first making sure that Kabumpo was not looking he took out his pencil and wrote: "Please take us to the castle of the Red Jinn, *at once!*" Underlining "at once," he stuffed the paper into the Post Man's box and feeling rather frightened ran after the Elegant Elephant. As he reached him, there was a great whirl and swish and his hand was gripped firmly by the wooden fingers of the Post Man. At the same moment Kabumpo's trunk was unceremoniously seized by the Guide Post Man's other hand and up like roman candles shot the three before Kabumpo even knew what was happening to him. Over the Emerald City and on they flashed, till Randy lost all sense of time, space and distance.

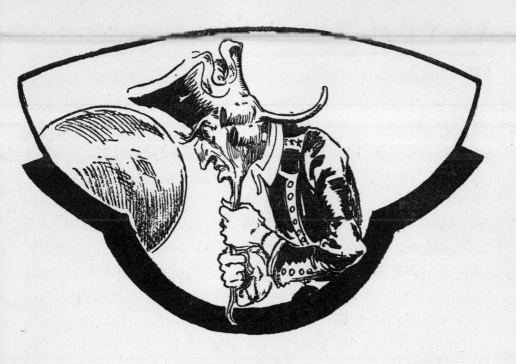

CHAPTER 10

Regalia

IN the far northwestern corner of the Gilliken country lies Regalia, a proud, pompous and regal little kingdom, high in the purple mountains of Oz. Its rulers, born to the purple, so to speak, have come down in straight succession for more than a thousand years and its castle, with amethyst windows and spires, is one of the most splendid sights in the country. The Regalians, though of a somewhat proud and haughty bearing, are really kind and merry at heart—much given to feasting, celebrations and gay processions.

But on this particular bright May morning an unwonted gloom hung over the mountainside. All the silver curtains in the castle were drawn and the courtiers, whispering uneasily among themselves, tiptoed up and down the silent corridors. Outside, the purple and regally clad mountaineers and villagers gathered in anxious groups and knots, and glancing up at the castle on the mountain top from time to time, shook their heads mournfully. The Royal Flag of Regalia was not flying from the tower, for the Royal Ruler of all the Regalians was absent from the castle and none knew when he would return —or whether he would return at all.

In the throne room, gazing intently at a great amethyst ball placed before him on a golden table, sat Hoochafoo, uncle of the absent ruler. Tugging anxiously at his purple beard he would look up now and then to cast worried glances at the door and windows. Hoochafoo, though not noted for his wit or wisdom, though dubbed by his mischievous compatriots Hoochafoo, the Foolish, was nevertheless a gentle and amiable old nobleman. But the responsibility of ruling Regalia weighed heavily upon his spirits, and anxiety over his Royal nephew made him still more nervous and unhappy.

"This suspense is killing me!" groaned the poor fellow, and running across the room he pulled the bell cord violently. "Summon the Wise Man, at once!" he directed the page who appeared to answer the bell. "At once!" And thrusting his long hands into the pockets of his splendid coat, Hoochafoo began pacing up and down the room at such a rate that he often met himself in the middle before he reached the end and when the old Wise Man did appear he almost knocked him over.

"Prunes and pretzels!" sputtered the sage, straightening his peaked cap. "What now? Your Highness knows this is my day for reflecting. How can I think of ways and means, I mean means and ways, bosh and bother what do I mean?"

"Sit down," begged Hoochafoo, flinging himself disconsolately upon the throne. "Sit down, you must stay with me. Ah, Chalulu, Chalulu, what shall I do, do?"

"Do nothing," answered the Wise Man, lowering himself crossly into a gold rocker. "There is nothing you can do, as I have told you a dozen times a day, nothing to do but wait until the conditions of the test have been fulfilled and the prince has proved his prowess, whatever that is," finished the Wise Man, with a furious sniff.

"Yes, but he may be in great danger," wailed

Hoochafoo, clasping and unclasping his hands, "facing unknown and savage monsters—lying exhausted at the bottom of some deep ravine. We must do something, I tell you. Call out the guard, search the forest! *Do* something, do you hear?"

"I hear," answered Chalulu sourly, "but I can do nothing. It is the law and written in the Royal Book of Regalia that the prince of the realm must go forth alone and unaided and prove himself worthy of the crown. *Alone*! Since the King, your brother, has chosen to retire from the throne and pursue the life of a hermit in the mountains, the prince must take his place. But why fret and worry this way? Have not all our former princes successfully passed the test? Has not our present prince shown himself brave and resourceful? Calm yourself, I beg. Go catch fish—catch cold—fall down the mountain," he suggested helpfully.

"But eight days, and not one word from him," moaned Hoochafoo, scarcely hearing the words of the Wise Man. "Not once has the amethyst ball flashed fire. Not one of the conditions of the test has been accomplished. Just read them again," he commanded, leaning his head wearily back against the throne and closing his eyes. Grumbling with annoyance, Chalulu unrolled and read a long scroll:

"Upon the passing, abdication or retirement of the King of Regalia, the prince of the realm shall go forth alone and without knowing the contents of this scroll fulfill all of its conditions.

133

"One: The prince must make three true friends.

"Two: He must faithfully serve a strange King.

"Three: He must save a Queen.

"Four: He must prove his bravery in battle.

"Five: He must overcome a monster.

"Six: He must disenchant a princess.

"Seven: He must receive from a wizard some magic treasure.

"As each test is successfully met the amethyst ball in the throne room will flash fire."

"Awful!" muttered Hoochafoo, as Chalulu finished reading and rolled up the scroll. "Ridiculous! How can *one* small prince do all that? Or even half of that? How—*how*? Why, he has done it! Look! Look! The ball has flashed fire! He has actually accomplished one of the feats. The prince is safe! Ring the bells! Call the guards! Declare a holiday at once! The prince is safe and alive and everything will be punjanoobias." The Wise Man, as Hoochafoo dashed hilariously to and fro, ringing bells, throwing up windows and pulling back the curtains, hurried anxiously after him.

"Remember, he has only passed one of the tests," wheezed Chalulu warningly. "There are still six more ahead of him."

"Six more? Six more fiddlesticks! If he has accomplished one, he will accomplish all. Don't you realize that this means the prince is safe and well? Stay here, you old skin and bones. Watch that ball while I go and break the good tidings to our countrymen!"

Rushing out on the balcony Hoochafoo flung up his arms and called out the happy news at the top of his lungs. And soon the cheers and joyous shouts of the Regalians rang from peak to peak so that the goats stopped their grazing and pricking up their ears turned their heads curiously toward the castle on the purple mountain top.

CHAPTER 11

In the Castle of the Red Jinn

ALTHOUGH their dash through the air seemed hours long to Randy and Kabumpo, just ten minutes after they left the Quadling Country of Oz, they had zipped over the Deadly Desert and come crashing down in Ev. Before them stretched a green and glassy sea and on the edge of the sea rose a scintillating red glass palace. Without waiting for them to rest or recover their breath, the Guide Post

Man, who seemed to have the strength of an army, dragged them to the palace, up its hundred glittering glass steps, through the doors and straight into the throne room. As soon as they had reached the throne, the Post Man dropped Randy's hand and Kabumpo's trunk as suddenly as he had seized them, and leaning wearily against a red glass pillar, closed his eyes.

"Such manners!" raged the Elegant Elephant, pressing his trunk to his head, which was still spinning giddily from the dizzy spin through the air. "Such manners!"

"Well, at least he brought us here!" panted Randy, pulling down his coat and smoothing back his pompadore. "I told him to take us to the castle of the Red Jinn and here we are. This must be his palace, Kabumpo. Everything is red!" The floors of the throne room were of smooth, transparent red glass; curtains of strung red rubies twinkled pleasantly at the windows and doors, and the tables, chairs and other furnishings were of shining crimson lacquer. A pleasant pink incense hung in the air and leading to the throne was a double row of enormous red vases. A smaller vase occupied the throne itself and giving the Elegant Elephant a nudge Randy whispered excitedly, "Look, look, there's the Red Jinn himself."

"I see nothing but a big red jug," wheezed Kabumpo, trying to focus his eyes on the throne. His head was still going round like a top.

"Sh—hh, not so loud! If we want him to help us we'll have to be careful!

"It's the Red Jinn, I tell you! Don't you see his arms and legs?" But flying had put the Elegant Elephant in a terrible temper and dragging his cloak straight he muttered crossly:

"Help us! Why shouldn't he help us? I guess our castle's as good as this, and I'm sure I'm as important as he is! Hum, humph, *ha*!"

"Har! Har! Har!" Kabumpo and Randy exchanged startled glances, for the muffled laughter had come from the middle of the red vase. Then up went the lid and out popped the round rosy face of an exceedingly fat and jolly old gentleman. The lid of the vase sat gaily on the back of his head like a cap and except for his red glass eyes, he looked quite kind, good-natured and grandfatherly. While Randy was trying to think of something polite to say, the old gentleman started the conversation himself by crying in a cheery voice:

OUT POPPED A ROUND, ROSY FACE

"The Jinn came out of his ginger jar
And observed to the company, 'How odd you are!
Hee, hee! Hoo, hoo! How odd! Har, har!'"

"Came by post, didn't you?" He paused to look curiously at the Guide Post Man who opened one eye, grinned and waved both arms at the Jinn. "Post haste, ho, ho!" chuckled the little wizard delightedly. "How long are you going to stay? I see you have brought a trunk." Pursing his lips and leaning over so far that he almost fell out of his jug, the Red Jinn stared mischievously at Kabumpo and then turned to wink at Randy.

"How could I come without my trunk?" hissed Kabumpo angrily. "It's part of me and you well know it!"

"You wouldn't part with it I suppose?" asked the Jinn solemnly. Kabumpo was too outraged to answer, so the Jinn went on quite cheerfully. "Then keep it by all means, my dear old Wackajamia for:

"It belongs to you and it's long enough
To hold a barrel of tea or snuff,
And if you took one sniff of snuff
You'd sneeze your head off, like enough."

"You're talking through your lid," stormed Ka-

bumpo, his small eyes beginning to bulge danger-
ously. "I am the Elegant Elephant of Oz and
Pumperdink, Prince and Regent in the House of
Pompus the Great and—"

"Who cares? Who cares? Har, har! Who cares?"
Folding his hands calmly over the vase encasing his
bulging body, the Red Jinn blinked his eyes sleepily. "Do you know any new jokes, stories or riddles?
Come, make yourselves agreeable and try to act like
visitors."

"Oh, please," interrupted Randy, afraid that the
Jinn's jokes and Kabumpo's temper would ruin
everything. "We have come to ask your help—!"

"Help? Help! Hel-lup!" shouted the Jinn, banging
on his jar with a red umbrella he had picked up from
the arm of the throne. "Help!" At his loud cries, in
from every direction poured huge black slaves in red
trousers and turbans. "Well," yawned the Jinn in a
bored voice, "here's the help, nearly all that I have.
Ask them whatever you wish!" Waving his arms
carelessly toward his men, he retired within himself
and closed the lid. The slaves, after touching their
noses once to the floor, looked expectantly toward
the travelers, but Kabumpo, snorting with disgust,
was already waddling furiously toward the door.

"Let's go," he muttered thunderously. "Let us leave this miserable palace at once. I've never been so insulted in my life. Help! Help, indeed!"

"But, Kabumpo!" cried Randy, tugging at the Elegant Elephant's robe. "Remember, this Jinn is the only one who can help us disenchant the King. You're not going to spoil everything, are you?"

"Spoil everything?" snapped Kabumpo, flapping his ears indignantly. "Do you expect me to stand here and make a fool of myself to amuse that old potted goose, yonder?"

"He's only in fun," explained Randy, speaking low so the Jinn could not hear. "Come on back and let's try again." Feeling in his heart that Randy was right, Kabumpo sniffed three times to show his contempt, then turned round and walked stiffly back to the throne. The slaves, receiving no orders or directions of any kind, had melted out of sight, the Post Man was sound asleep against the red pillar and there was no sound at all in the great, glittering room. The ruby-handled umbrella still lay on the arm of the throne and taking it in his hand, Randy tapped gently on the Jinn's jar. So quickly that the boy almost toppled over backwards the Jinn thrust up his head.

"My mercy me!" puffed the little old fellow merrily. "You still here?"

"Yes!" answered Randy quickly, and before the Jinn had time to make any more jokes. "We wanted to tell you a story, sir."

"What kind of a story?" Without stopping to explain, while Kabumpo shifted sulkily from one foot to the other, Randy began at once a recital of all that had happened in Pumperdink and how Faleero and Kettywig had plotted to steal Pompus' throne. When he came to the part where Faleero, disguised as a traveling magician, had persuaded the royal family to pick the fire roses from the mist tree and how they had instantly vanished from view, the Jinn bounced up and spun round three times on his left heel.

"Red magic! I know how she did that," he exclaimed triumphantly. "And I am the only wizard in the north who can restore their Majesties."

"That's just what the soothsayer told us, that's just why we came to you." Quickly finishing up the story of their travels through Oz and their flight to Ev with the Post Man, Randy stepped closer and looked right into the Jinn's face. "You will help us, won't you?" he asked coaxingly.

"Help us and you shall have all of these jewels, my good fellow," added Kabumpo condescendingly. Feeling in his pocket, he pulled out a plump bag and held it haughtily up in his trunk. The Jinn, who had been on the point of answering Randy, looked in

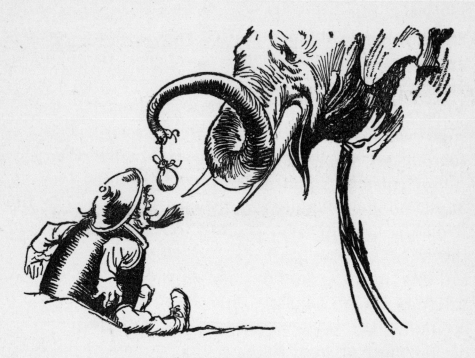

astonishment at the little bag. An expression of anger and disgust crossed his ruddy face and snatching up his red umbrella he waved it three times round his head. As Randy gasped and Kabumpo stepped back, fifty blacks came racing into the throne room. Each bore a great basket of blazing rubies. These they set down before their master and grinning wickedly at Kabumpo retired like shadows through the curtains. The Jinn, without another look at the Elegant Elephant or the little Gilliken sank out of sight.

"Now you've done it! Now you've done it and ruined everything! Great Gillikens, he has more jewels than we've seen in the whole of our lives! Whatever made you do that, Kabumpo? Whatever shall we do now?" Randy flung himself disconsolately on a red laquered sofa.

"Do what you like. I'm through!" Looking very huge and haughty, but feeling very small and foolish, Kabumpo started to leave the Jinn's palace. As the Elegant Elephant went swishing through the tinkling red curtains, Randy rose and stood uncertainly before the owner of the palace. Did he dare speak to him again? While he was still trying to decide, the Guide Post Man suddenly awoke and in one tremendous leap covered the distance between the red pillar and the throne. Raising his wooden arms, he brought them down so hard on the Jinn's jar that the Jinn almost rolled off his spun glass cushions. Seizing the arm of the throne to save

145

himself, the little wizard stuck out his head and rolled his eyes savagely from side to side. As they lit upon the Post Man, that strange individual took off his knob, bowed politely and waving first one arm and then the other, whizzed out of an open window.

"I guess he wanted to say good-bye," ventured Randy in an embarrassed voice.

"And good riddance, too," grumbled the Jinn crossly. "Has that elephant gone?"

"I—I don't think so," answered Randy uncomfortably. "You see, we thought you might change your mind about helping us."

"Help you? Why should I help you?" demanded the Jinn in a red peppery voice. "Give me one good reason if you can."

"There really isn't any reason," admitted Randy, shaking his head ruefully. "But you are the only one wise, skillful and powerful enough to do it and I thought you might like the fun of trying."

"It would be fun," mused the Jinn, half to himself and half to Randy. "I haven't been anywhere for a hundred years. Where is this Pumperdinky kingdom anyway and what relation are you to its unhappy sovereigns?"

"None at all," Randy told him frankly. "But I

was in the castle when all this happened and as I'm fond of mysteries and like Kabumpo, I thought it would be a fine adventure to help restore the royal family to the throne."

"But that elephant is perfectly preposterous!"

exploded the Jinn indignantly. "Offering me a peanut bag full of jewels. Me, the real and only Red Jinn in all Ev, possessor of fifty ruby mines and all the science and secrets of red magic and art!"

"Oh, he didn't mean to offend you, I'm sure," explained Randy anxiously. "He's grand, really, when he's not showing off. You'll like him a lot when you know him better."

"Well, I like *you* a lot now," smiled the Jinn, twinkling his glass eyes at the boy. "And I believe I'll help you, too. Shake hands on it, Randy. That's what you call yourself, is it not? And to my friends my name is Jinnicky,

> "He's the one and only Jinnicky and very awfully finicky
> About his friends, his jewels, his tea;
> So try to please him, boy, or he
> Will seal you in a ginger jar and toss you in the sea,
>   Har, har!
> How har, har, horrid that would be, so let's forget it.
>   Where's my tea?"

The last line Jinnicky roared so loud that the very curtains trembled and before Randy could blink, a small servitor, bearing a silver tea tray flashed down before the throne. Handing Randy one cup and the Jinn another, he set down the tray and retired as quickly as he had appeared. Perched on the edge of a red chair, Randy sipped the steaming liquid, recalling rather uneasily the verses about the ginger jar. He was worried about Kabumpo, too. But the

Red Jinn, chattering away of Pumperdink and the art of restoring the vanished ones, seemed to have forgotten everything unpleasant and was so jolly, and bubbling over with good humor that Randy began to feel gay and light-hearted himself.

"When will we start?" he asked eagerly. "Now?"

"Now, or never!" beamed Jinnicky, setting down his tea cup and bouncing off the throne. "Where is that big gom of an elephant, anyway?"

149

CHAPTER 12

The Grand Advizier Advises

THEY found Kabumpo under a ginger tree in the garden and when Jinnicky clapped him briskly on the trunk and told him he had decided to help him, the Elegant Elephant was so embarrassed that he could do nothing but grunt and splutter. Taking these dubious sounds for appreciation and thanks, the Jinn announced that they were leaving for Pumperdink at once, and motioning for

Kabumpo to follow pattered determinedly back to the palace.

"There are always three things to decide about a journey," panted Jinnicky, dropping down on his cushions and clasping his hands round his shiny middle. "Where to go, what to take and how to travel. The first we know, the second we shall leave to my Grand Advizier, the third we must decide for ourselves. Now then, my lads, how shall we travel to Pumperdink?"

"Where's the Post Man?" demanded Kabumpo, looking around sharply. He had not enjoyed the dash through the air with their singular guide, but he had rather counted on going back the same way. "Where is that surly offspring of a tree stump?"

"Gone," answered Jinnicky, calmly rocking back and forth. "So we cannot go by post. My magic jinrikisha might carry Randy and me but it would never hold an elephant, so we cannot go by jinrikisha."

"I should not care to ride in a jinrikisha anyway," sniffed Kabumpo loftily. "I've never ridden in such a contrivance, and I don't intend to begin now."

"Then it looks as though we would have to go afoot," mused Jinnicky, taking off his lid and scratch-

151

ing his red head reflectively. "Mercy me!" He looked ruefully at his small, fat, slippered feet and sighed.

"Oh, you can ride on my back, I suppose," remarked Kabumpo carelessly. He had no great liking for the saucy little Jinn, but felt he must put up with some inconveniences if he was to get him to Pumperdink and save the kingdom from Kettywig. "Of course, if you fall off and jar yourself, you cannot hold me responsible," he added in a severe tone. "And if that does happen," thought Kabumpo spitefully to himself, "I shall just take his magic and disenchant their Majesties without his help."

Randy looked distressed at Kabumpo's rude speech, but the Jinn, who loved a joke, even on himself, laughed uproariously.

"You cannot jar a fellow who is already jarred," puffed Jinnicky, wiping the tears of merriment from his fat cheeks. "I've been jarred all my life and never been broken yet." The Jinn winked a glass eye at Kabumpo, and the Elegant Elephant was so upset to have the Jinn read his thoughts that he immediately lapsed into an uneasy silence.

"But how about the Deadly Desert?" asked Randy, sitting down on the steps of Jinnicky's throne and looking up eagerly into his face.

"Oh—that!" Jinnicky snapped his fingers unconcernedly. "Wait till we come to it, my boy." Taking
up his red umbrella he pounded vigorously on the
arm of his ruby throne. In answer to this strange
summons, a tall, turbaned and exceedingly dignified
gentleman stalked into his presence. He was taste-
fully dressed in red, had a neat pointed nose, a neat
pointed beard and the toes of his neat pointed shoes
curled nearly up to his knees. With folded arms he
approached the throne, and nodding in a careless
fashion to the Jinn stood waiting for him to speak.
This Jinnicky did at once by explaining cheerfully:

"Alibabble, these are my friends from Oz—Kabumpo and Randy. I leave you to guess which name
belongs to which." Alibabble, raising one eyebrow,
glanced quickly from the Elegant Elephant to the
little Gilliken and with a haughty and supercilious
nod turned back to his master.

"You sent for me?" he observed in an annoyed
voice.

"Yes, I'm going on a journey. Kindly make the
necessary preparations." Jinnicky rubbed his hands
gleefully together.

"Well, first, I advise you to have a hair cut," said
Alibabble, in a firm voice.

153

"A hair cut!" shrieked the Jinn angrily. "You're always telling me to have my hair cut. I'll cut your salary for this. No wonder I want to get away. Hair cut! Hair cut! I hear nothing else from morning till night. Barber! Barber!" Jinnicky sprang

to his feet, his glass eyes rolling savagely. And when the barber, attired in the same red costume as Alibabble, arrived, breathless from his hurry, the Jinn waved sternly at the Grand Advizier.

"Cut his hair and just take off the head with it,"

he commanded temperishly. As the barber drew a
long gleaming scimitar from his sash, Randy jumped
up in horror and even Kabumpo gave a grunt of
protest. Alibabble, however, seemed perfectly calm.
Seating himself in a red chair, be began slowly un-

winding his turban, disclosing a crop of shortly
clipped red hair. As the barber raised his scimitar
the Red Jinn seemed to think of something.

"Never mind about his head," he mumbled disagreeably, "I might need it later." Randy could not

help thinking Alibabble might need it himself, but the Grand Advizier, without a change of expression, sat quietly smoking a cheroot while the barber shaved off what was left of his short locks.

"Well, now that we've had our hair cut," smiled Jinnicky maliciously, "let us proceed with the rest of the preparations."

"Are you going to take Addie?" inquired Alibabble, picking up a small basket from a red stand.

"I don't—know—" murmured the Jinn, rubbing his chin as he deliberated. "Do you think there'll be much adding to do, Randy?"

"Adding!" exclaimed the boy, as the Grand Advizier took the top off the basket. "Oh, I don't think so, sir. Do you, Kabumpo?"

"How should I know?" sniffed the Elegant Elephant, swinging his trunk indifferently. Then his eyes popped out in real astonishment, as a small snake that had been coiled in the basket rose up on its tail and lazily surveyed him.

"Then she can help us now," decided the Jinn, settling back contentedly, "and add up all the articles we need for the journey. She's my hissing adder," he confided pridefully to Randy. "No sum is too difficult for her, either."

The Grand Advizier addressed the adder in a dignified tone. "Let me see, now. We'll need the green jug, the blue vase, the red jar, the black pitcher, the purple incense, the yellow incense, the pink incense, the blue bottle, the green bottle, the grey bottle, the red bottle, the green flower pot, your red glasses, the silver dinner bell and your old umbrella."

As the Grand Advizier counted off each item, Addie gave a hiss and made a puncture on a sheet of paper suspended from the handle of the basket with her sharp tongue. Randy was so interested watching the hissing adder at work that he paid no attention at all to what Alibabble was saying. But Kabumpo, putting his great ears inquisitively forward began to seethe and bubble with resentment and indignation.

"Pots! Bottles, jugs and flower pots! Does he take us for peddlers?" fumed Kabumpo fiercely in Randy's ear. "Great grump! I'll look like a pack horse.

"How about some food?" he called, belligerently raising his trunk.

"There will be food," announced Alibabble composedly, "but not your kind of food, my friend. I fear you will have to forage for your provisions."

"Forage?" trumpeted Kabumpo, with an outraged snort. "What forage?"

> "Har, har! You must forage for elephant porridge,
> For cabbage and turnips and round nuts,
> For the grasses and hay you will need every day,
> For the tree leaves and tea leaves and ground nuts!"

chanted Jinnicky, leaning over to take the paper from Addie. The hissing adder had placed a line of dots under her list and punctured out with her tongue the figure fifteen. While the Jinn examined this figure with wrinkled brows and Kabumpo rumbled angrily under his breath, Alibabble shut Addie up in the basket, snatched the paper from Jinnicky and was gone. In exactly five minutes by the Jinn's red glass clock, two of the Jinn's tallest slaves appeared carrying the fifteen bottles, jugs, pots and vases. A third little black walked behind them and handing Jinnicky a silver bell, a pair of red glasses and a note, promptly took to his heels. The Jinn gave the bell and spectacles to Randy and pursing up his lips opened the note.

"I earnestly advise your Majesty to have a hair cut before starting on this journey." It was signed "Alibabble," and Randy, who had read the message surreptitiously over Jinnicky's shoulder, skipped quickly down the steps.

"Hair cut! Hair cut! There he goes again!" fumed the Red Jinn fretfully. "Do you really think my hair is too long?" Randy measured the distance between himself and the door and then spoke up boldly:

"It is a little long, your Highness."

"It's long enough to plait and tie with ribbons," grunted Kabumpo, snatching Randy down the last step of the throne as Jinnicky began to call for the barber. But this time, when the barber appeared, he actually let the fellow cut his hair, groaning

159

terribly as each lock fell under the shears and looking so reproachfully at Randy that the boy felt quite
guilty and uncomfortable. But at last the disagreeable operation was over and Jinnicky, jumping to
his feet, summoned three of his favorite servitors.
These handy fellows quickly rigged up a cushioned
seat for the Jinn on Kabumpo's back with a neat
rope ladder to help him up and down. The bottles
and jugs were stowed in two wicker baskets and
slung over the Elegant Elephant's shoulders. Then
Randy mounted to his favorite place back of Kabumpo's left ear, the Jinn ran up the rope ladder
and fell breathlessly among the cushions of his seat
and Kabumpo, lifting his trunk, gave such a trumpet
that a double line of courtiers drawn up to wish
Jinnicky farewell tumbled over like ten pins. Then
the Elegant Elephant charged like a hurricane out
of the red glass palace. Jinnicky's subjects, clad in
towering turbans and loose red trousers, waved
cheerfully as they swept through the glittering
streets of the red city, and the red glass guns in the
fortress fired a salute of twenty glass cannon balls
as they passed through the sparkling city gates.

"They seem to think a lot of you," called Randy,
when he could make himself heard.

"THEY SEEM TO THINK A LOT OF YOU," CALLED RANDY

161

"Doubtless! Doubtless," answered Jinnicky, with a little sniff of satisfaction. "People grow terribly fond of you when they find you are about to depart."

"But who'll rule the country without you?" asked Randy, looking over his shoulder at the Jinn.

"Alibabble, I dare say, and well enough, too. Mercy me! I'll be glad to be rid of the fellow for a while. He's always telling me something I already know."

"As you know so much, possibly you can tell me the shortest route to Oz," puffed Kabumpo, looking impatiently around at Jinnicky.

"To tell the truth, I know very little about roads," confessed Jinnicky. "Traveling swiftly through the air in my magic jinrikisha I see very few of them. However, I believe the road we are on now leads directly to the Deadly Desert."

"So you travel very fast in that magic jinrikisha?" murmured Kabumpo, in a tone Randy did not quite like. "Very fast. Ha! Well, how's this?" The Jinn, as you can well imagine, made no answer. All he could do was hold on to the arms of his wicker seat, blink, groan and gasp and whisper magic words and incantations for his safety and protection. Randy, with both hands twisted securely in the Elegant Ele-

162

phant's collar, blew out and waved like a banner. Traveling at top speed on an elephant is like riding a stormy sea in a small boat. And how far or how long they tore through the wild rocky country of Ev, neither Randy nor the Red Jinn could have told

you. Even the Elegant Elephant himself did not know, but soon the hot, stinging scent of burning sand made him slow down and peering through a thin fringe of trees ahead he came to a sudden and unceremonious stop.

"Something will turn up," said the Red Jinn

164

"Well, here's your desert," he announced carelessly. "And now that we are here, what are you going to do about it?" The Jinn, who had withdrawn into his jar like a turtle into its shell, popped up his head and looked cautiously about.

"Why, it is the desert," said Jinnicky, sniffing the sulphurous air fastidiously. "Mercy me!" Randy thought it quite sporting of the Jinn to say nothing of the awful shaking he had endured. He, himself, was stiff and sore and extremely provoked at Kabumpo.

"Have you any magic in those baskets that will help us to cross the desert?" he asked anxiously.

"No!" answered the Jinn frankly. "I haven't. But I'll probably think of something before long."

"Before long?" squealed Kabumpo indignantly. "Do you realize that the King, Queen, Prince and Princesses of Pumperdink are in dire and awful danger and need your help at once?"

"Keep your skin on! Keep your skin on!" advised Jinnicky calmly. "Vanishing is neither dangerous nor awful. On the contrary it is quite pleasant and restful. You ought to try it some time. So just have patience and something will turn up to help us cross this desert. Just see if it doesn't." Folding his hands the Jinn settled back contentedly against his cushions. Even Randy began to feel a little annoyed at this. The idea of waiting on the edge of the desert for something to turn up seemed utterly foolish and ridiculous to him. As for Kabumpo, he was so put out that he snatched up a small tree by the roots and swallowed it whole.

"Something will come along soon," repeated Jinnicky, blinking his red glass eyes sleepily. "Look —something's coming up now!" He turned a fat pink finger toward the sky which was turning a leaden and thunderous grey.

"A storm!" gasped Kabumpo, staring worriedly at the darkening clouds. "A storm's coming up. Great grump, what good will that do?"

CHAPTER 13

The Red Jinn's Looking Glasses

A LONG, threatening rumble of thunder sent the Elegant Elephant on a quick rush for cover, but there was in all that dreary waste land, not a tree, rock or shack of any kind to shelter them. Jinnicky, after a second look at the sky, handed his umbrella to Randy and ducked into his jar; and just in time, too, for the rain fell in torrents and the wind rose to such a gale that Kabumpo swayed

167

like a ship in a storm and Randy found it impossible to put up the red umbrella. There was a great deal to be said for Jinnicky's jar, for he had not only drawn in his head, but his arms and legs as well, and was perfectly dry and secure while Kabumpo and Randy shivered with wet and discomfort. Looking at him enviously, the boy wondered how it would feel to be so strangely and magically constructed. The wind howled fearfully, Kabumpo's ears flapped like sails in the blast and conversation of any kind was simply impossible.

"If that Post Man had not gone off we might have been in Pumperdink by this time," thought Randy sadly, "and now, dear knows whether we shall ever get there." But the storm, as quickly as it had risen, passed. The sky turned grey, then pink and though it was still raining the sun came out and a rainbow burst suddenly through the clouds.

"Oh, look!" called Randy, pointing to the vivid arch of light. But Kabumpo, paying no attention to the rainbow, shook himself so vigorously that the Jinn rattled in his jar and all the jugs and vases jingled noisily together.

"Very pretty, no doubt," sniffed Kabumpo shortly, "but this is no time to look for rainbows, my boy.

Our clothes are ruined, you'll probably catch pneumonia and *how* are we to cross this grumpy desert? A fine help this Jinn's been! I'll bet he just came for the ride."

"Sh—hh!" warned Randy anxiously. "Don't you remember, he can hear through his lid. Oh, look! Look! Do look, Kabumpo, the rainbow's coming right down to the edge of the rocks and there's a girl or a fairy dancing on the rim."

"Why, it's Polychrome!" exclaimed Kabumpo, his interest aroused at last. "It's the rainbow's daughter. She has often visited in Oz. Polly! Polly, my dear, come on down and let's have a look at you."

"I told you something would turn up," observed Jinnicky, popping out his head. "Next time, maybe, you'll believe me." Randy was much too interested in the little sky fairy to pay any attention to Jinnicky. Though she seemed to be a maid of mist and light, Polychrome was at the same time as real and as lovely as the lovliest of Oz maidens. Dancing down the rainbow, she jumped off the end, skipped lightly across the rocks and seated herself cozily in the bend of the Elegant Elephant's trunk.

"Hello, Kabumpo, aren't you a long way from home?" she asked affectionately.

169

"A very long way," admitted the Elegant Elephant glumly. "But it's a long, long story, my dear!"

"Just like your nose," laughed Polly mischievously. "Well, I like long noses and stories and—travelers." She smiled gaily up at Randy and the Red Jinn as Kabumpo pompously introduced them, and in less time than it has taken me to write one page of this story, Kabumpo had explained the whole reason and purpose of their journey.

"And the sooner we reach Pumperdink, the sooner the Red Jinn can restore the royal family," put in Randy, as Kabumpo paused for breath. "But we cannot cross this desert, so here we are!"

"Why, that's easy!" Polly jumped to the ground with a little laugh. "I'll just lend you my rainbow. See—!" She stretched her arms up gleefully. "It arches all the way across and all you have to do is follow me."

"But I'm too heavy! I'd fall through—or off, or puncture it," objected Kabumpo nervously.

"Or get rainbow-legged," chuckled the Red Jinn, who had been quiet as long as he could manage. "The plain truth is, you're afraid. Why not admit it?"

"Ha!" raged Kabumpo, and with a furious glance

at Jinnicky stamped after Polychrome, who had already stepped up on the bow and was beckoning for them to follow.

Randy, it must be confessed, shared Kabumpo's misgivings, and as they approached the misty and fragile arch he shivered with something besides cold and dampness. They would certainly fall through, fall on the deadly desert and vanish as utterly as the King of Pumperdink. But Polychrome and the Red Jinn seemed so gay and indifferent that the mountain boy resolved to perish manfully, and as Kabumpo stepped up on the rainbow, he began to whistle an old Gilliken jig.

The rainbow slanted gradually at the start and as Kabumpo cautiously started upward, his feet seemed scarcely to touch the iridescent path of light. But for all its transparency, the rainbow proved sturdy as steel. It was like crossing the desert on some unreal and airy bridge, and with Polychrome dancing ahead Kabumpo quickly and safely reached the center. Here Polly bade them an affectionate farewell and regretfully Randy waved good-bye to the little sky fairy. Going down was more difficult than going up and though the Elegant Elephant held back and braced his legs as best he could, he found himself running faster and faster. So fast, in fact, did he run that everything grew blurred and when he came to the end of the rainbow he plunged off and ran for half a mile before he could stop himself.

"Very neat," approved Jinnicky, straightening his lid, which had fallen over one ear. "And this, I suppose, is the famous Winkie country of Oz!"

"Tell me something I don't already know," grunted Kabumpo, still panting from his dash down the rainbow. "Of course it's the Winkie country. Isn't everything yellow?"

"Everything excepting you,
And you, old El, seem rather blue,

though I don't see why," said Jinnicky, with a wink at Randy. "That rainbow was a very pleasant solution of a very unpleasant difficulty."

"I wish Polychrome had come with us," sighed Randy. "Do you know her very well, Kabumpo?"

"As well as anyone ever knows a fairy," answered Kabumpo, squinting up at the sky, where the rainbow was just melting out of sight. "But now," he concluded briskly, "we must find the shortest route to Pumperdink. Let—me—see!" Kabumpo flapped his big ears and blinked across the valley.

172

"Since you know so much about the Winkie country, that surely will not be difficult," teased Jinnicky, folding his hands complacently.

"Oh, dear!" thought Randy, as Kabumpo glared over his shoulder at the little Jinn, "I do wish they'd stop snapping at each other this way. They're both so nice separately. Why can't they be nice together?" To save the Elegant Elephant's honor and reputation, he began to peer around anxiously for signs of a road or highway. But as far as he could see there were nothing but plains, hills and forests. Not a road, nor a house, nor even a castle! As Kabumpo swayed uncertainly from left to right, Jinnicky leaned forward and touched Randy on the shoulder.

"Just hand me my red glasses, will you?" he muttered hurriedly. Randy had put the Jinn's silver bell and glasses in his pocket and now, without thinking much about it, he handed Jinnicky his specs. Clapping them on his nose, Jinnicky clambered down the rope ladder and began hurrying as fast as his fat little feet would carry him toward a deep and dangerous looking forest.

"Stop! What are you doing? Where are you going?" roared Kabumpo, lunging angrily after him. Much as the Red Jinn annoyed him, he did not intend to let him get away at this stage of the journey. "Come back! Come back!" he trumpeted loudly. "Do you want to ruin your shoes?" he puffed, as he caught up with the strange little figure.

"No, not especially," answered the Jinn, squinting over his shoulder at the Elegant Elephant. "I'm looking for the road to Pumperdink and this is the only way to find it."

"How do you expect to find the road when you

know nothing of this part of the country?" inquired Kabumpo sarcastically.

"I expect to find it with the help of these looking glasses," announced Jinnicky, tapping his red specs proudly. "They will look for anything I ask them to look for. See?" And elevating his little red nose, the Jinn ran determinedly on into the forest.

"M—mm! They must be magic glasses," breathed Randy, leaning forward eagerly.

"Well, all I say is—if he has to walk all the way to Pumperdink, he'll never get there and neither will we." Kabumpo spoke with conviction. "Look, he's tired already. Look at the old goose, will you?" Randy had to agree that Kabumpo was right, for Jinnicky had taken off his glasses and was leaning against a yellow oak fanning himself with his lid.

"Maybe he'll lend them to me," whispered Randy, as Kabumpo stopped beside the oak.

"What good will that do?" sighed the Elegant Elephant. "You can't walk much faster than he can. I am the one who should wear them."

"What's that?" asked Jinnicky, replacing his lid and glancing wearily up at Kabumpo.

"I said I was the one who should wear the looking glasses," repeated Kabumpo calmly. "I can travel

175

twenty times as fast as you can and at this rate we'll never get anywhere."

"Just what I was thinking," sniffed Jinnicky, much to Randy's surprise, for he always expected an argument when Kabumpo and the Jinn got into a conversation.

"But they won't fit," exclaimed Randy.

"My looking glasses will fit anyone, even an elephant," boasted Jinnicky, and before Kabumpo could change his mind or make any more remarks, he flung the red spectacles at his head. Instead of smashing to bits they sailed over the Elegant Elephant's great ears and settled quietly on his trunk, and unless you have ever seen an elephant wearing red looking glasses you have no idea how comical Kabumpo looked.

"Get aboard! Hurry up!" he wheezed excitedly, speaking out of the corner of his mouth. "They're beginning to tug me along like a magnet. Up with you! Quick, or you'll be left behind. Great grump, wherever am I going?" Jinnicky had just time to sieze the first rung of the rope ladder before Kabumpo started running like the wind through the yellow forest. Grasping Jinnicky's hand, Randy helped him to his seat and soon they were speeding

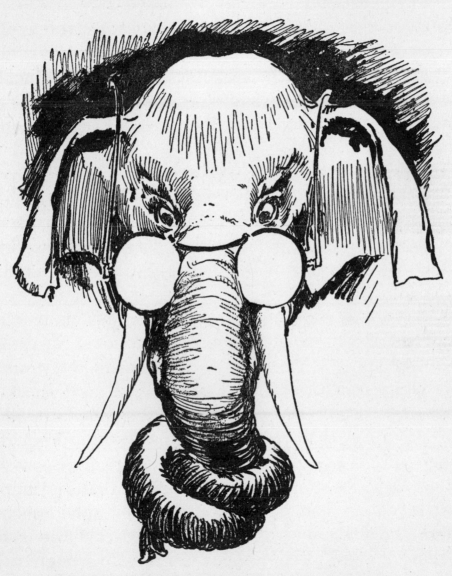

YOU HAVE NO IDEA HOW COMICAL KABUMPO LOOKED

along so swiftly that the trees flashed by like tele-graph poles when you ride in an express train. On the other side of the forest, the looking glasses had a little difficulty deciding which way to go; conse-quently the speed of the Elegant Elephant slackened down to a more comfortable pace.

"Whew!" whistled Randy, rubbing his eye with one hand and hanging on tight with the other. Then, glancing ahead, he gave a terrible start. A monster twice as large as Kabumpo, with a rhinoceros' head and a dragon's body, stood gnashing its tusks directly in their path.

"Stop!" quavered Jinnicky, waving his umbrella wildly.

"Stop!" begged Randy tugging at Kabumpo's ear. But Kabumpo, if he heard them, gave no heed, quick-ening his pace, if anything, so that it seemed to poor Randy that they were rushing right into the jaws of destruction, as, indeed they were. Clasping his small sword desperately, he was wondering what in Oz to do when Jinnicky, muttering and spluttering, crawled hurriedly past him and snatched the red looking glasses off Kabumpo's trunk. No sooner had he done so than Kabumpo stopped just in time to keep from impaling himself with the monster's horn, but not in time for Randy. The jolt of their sudden halt sent the boy flying into the air. With his sword clasped in both hands, he described a perfect arc and came crashing down on the horrible creature's neck. There was a cough, choke and gurgle—Randy had

just presence of mind enough to pull out his sword and jump aside when the monster rolled over on its back and lay still.

"Bravo! Bravo!" shrilled Jinnicky, waving his umbrella, while Kabumpo's eyes popped out with pride and admiration. "You have saved all our lives, my lad, and overcome the most formidable combinoceros I've ever had the misfortune to meet or lay eyes on!" Fairly tumbling down the ladder, the Red Jinn clasped Randy to his jar, showering him with praises and congratulations.

"Are you all right?" demanded Kabumpo anxiously, when Jinnicky finally let him go. "Great grump, what kind of rinkety-rank looking glasses are those? Couldn't stop till you dragged them off. They're dangerous, frightfully dangerous, that's what they are!" Jinnicky nodded soberly.

"That's why I didn't wear them when we first started," he explained quickly. "They would have rushed us right onto the Deadly Desert. One must wear my red looking glasses with very great care— very great care."

"I'm not sure I wish to wear them at all," shuddered Kabumpo, walking stiffly around the fallen monster. "Look at that horn! The King shall hear of this, my boy. You shall have twelve new suits and a velvet cloak when we reach Pumperdink."

Randy, who had destroyed the combinoceros more by good luck than good swordsmanship, tried to explain how he had fallen with his sword pointed downward on the animal's neck. But neither Jinnicky nor Kabumpo would listen to him, so he finally gave up and basked as any boy would in their expressions of pride and approval.

"How long will it lie here?" he asked, curiously touching the great beast with his foot. In any country but Oz, the monster would have been utterly dead and done for, but in Oz, there is no death. People and animals can be overcome for a time but not forever, so Randy felt a little uneasy.

"Well, I hope it does not recover in my lifetime," chuckled Jinnicky, climbing back to his comfortable seat, "and to be on the safe side, let us depart, get hence, and go forward!"

"The only safe side of that creature is the other side," rumbled Kabumpo distastefully. "The further we are from something worse, the nearer we are to something better."

"Har, har, har!" laughed Jinnicky, and when Kabumpo had put three hills and a little wood between them and the combinoceros, he called out cheerfully:

"How about dinner? The sun's going down and while we can still find our mouths we'd better eat."

"But what shall we eat?" asked Randy, looking

181

rather resentfully at the baskets of jugs and bottles that could so well have carried sandwiches and fruit.

"Just hand me my silver bell," directed the Jinn, with a broad wink. "Hand me the bell and all will be well!" Pulling the bell from his pocket, Randy passed it back to Jinnicky, and Jinnicky, with a mischievous smile, rang it three times.

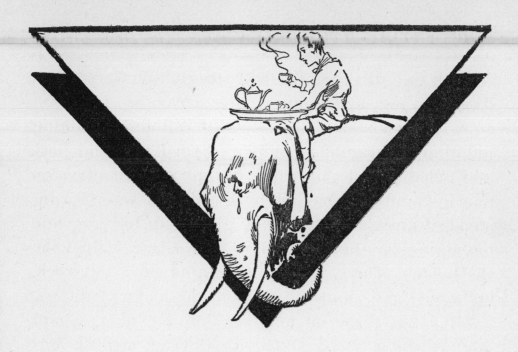

CHAPTER 14

King, King, Double King!

THE silvery note of the dinner bell had barely sounded before a small, turbaned slave flashed down from nowhere and set a well ordered dinner tray on the arm of Jinnicky's seat. Smiling amiably, he vanished but reappeared almost instantly, for the Red Jinn had rung the bell again. This time the little fellow brought a dinner for Randy and setting the tray carefully between Kabumpo's ears vanished away before the boy had time to thank him.

"Fall to," directed Jinnicky, as Randy stared in a dazed fashion at the appetizing array.

"Well, how about me?" shrilled Kabumpo, looking indignantly over his shoulder. "Am I to stand here and twiddle my trunk while you gorge yourselves on magic viands? What am I to eat and when?" Instead of answering, Jinnicky picked up his tray and motioning for Randy to follow backed carefully down the ladder. Then, placing his dinner on a flat rock, he turned and handed Kabumpo the looking glasses.

"Just put these on and go look for an elephant dinner," he advised jovially. "But be careful, terribly, dreadfully careful!" Remember the combinoceros!" The Elegant Elephant swayed doubtfully to and fro and then, as he really was starving, he clapped on the red specs and disappeared at a gallop.

"Now we can dine in quiet and peace," murmured Jinnicky, seating himself picnic fashion on the ground. "A handy thing, my magic dinner bell, eh, my lad?" Randy nodded, his mouth too full of roast duck to speak.

"I did have two of these dinner bells," went on Jinnicky, between rapid bites of biscuit, "but one was stolen and fell into the hands of a countryman of yours—Jack Pumpkinhead, I think he called himself."

"The Pumpkinhead who lives near the Emerald City?" asked Randy, in surprise. Jinnicky nodded his head vigorously. "The very same. Finding himself in some dire difficulty, this Jack fellow rang the bell, seized Ginger's hand when he appeared with the dinner tray and came back with him to my palace. So you see, you are not the only people who have appealed to me for help."

"Did you help Jack?" inquired Randy, with an interested little sniff.

"Yes," admitted the Jinn, slowly sipping his tea, "I saved three of his comrades from a magic sack, though I did not hear how it all turned out till a year later. That meddling little Wizard of Oz mixed his magic with mine and completely spoiled the affair for me."

"Well, I hope nobody meddles with your magic this time," sighed Randy, popping a large strawberry into his mouth and crunching it up with great relish.

"Kabumpo has all my magic at the present moment," mused Jinnicky a bit thoughtfully.

"Say, I hope nothing happens to Kabumpo!" Suddenly remembering that the Elegant Elephant wore the red looking glasses, Randy looked anxiously over at the Jinn. "Your specs may get him in trouble!"

"But he's not looking for trouble," observed Jinnicky calmly, "he's looking for dinner. Shall I ring for more duck, my boy?" Randy shook his head,

for he could not possibly have eaten another bite. As he jumped up to look around for Kabumpo both trays and dishes vanished into thin air and the Red Jinn, leaning back against a turnip tree, closed his eyes and began to hum an old Ev ballad. Randy had not gone more than a dozen steps nor the Jinn reached more than the second stanza before Kabumpo hove hilariously into view. Hay was sticking to him everywhere and he had evidently dined with more gusto than elegance. The looking glasses had led him directly to a farmer's granary and after eating several buckets of oats, bran and corn he had finished off with a stack of hay and almost pleasantly he took off the red spectacles and returned them to the Jinn.

"Did you see any cities or towns ahead?" asked Randy, picking the strands of hay off Kabumpo's jeweled collar and headpiece. "Did you find anything besides oats and beans?"

"There's a city on the other side of that second hill," announced Kabumpo importantly. "And if we hurry we might reach it before dark." So Jinnicky joyfully climbed into his high seat on Kabumpo's back, Randy ran up his trunk and off they started at the Elegant Elephant's best pace, reaching the top of the hill in almost no time. On top of the second hill they saw a shining yellow city. The houses were of smooth yellow stone with golden roofs. Splendid twin castles with golden spires stood above the cluster of cottages and shops, and the last rays

187

of the setting sun touched the castle towers and golden roofs with such a dazzling light that it seemed almost as if the city were afire. Blinking approval, for he loved all grandeur, Kabumpo started energetically toward the second hill and had got about

half way up, when a great band of musicians marched through the city gates and came down to meet them, playing such a lively air that it was all the Elegant Elephant could do to keep from dancing.

"They quite evidently take us for people of importance," said Jinnicky, setting his lid at a more stylish angle and dusting off his jar with a red silk handkerchief.

"And quite right, too," answered Kabumpo, tossing his head proudly. "We *are* people of great importance."

"To ourselves!" chuckled Jinnicky, to Randy's great amusement. "And this night I shall treat them to my most elegant snores." Kabumpo, pretending not to hear the Jinn's last remark, lifted his trunk in a grand salute as the leader of the golden band halted directly in their path. The musicians carried simply tremendous horns and flutes and wore striking uniforms and caps of white and yellow. That was the last thing Randy remembered. For, lifting his baton, the bandmaster gave a signal to his men, and with such a blare of trumpets that the Jinn's red hair stood straight on end carrying his lid up with it, the horns shot out fifteen feet (for they were of a trick and sliding variety) and knocked the travelers perfectly senseless—at least two of them.

One horn hit the Elegant Elephant such a blow between the eyes that he nearly fell to his knees; another shot between his ears and rolled Randy to the ground. Jinnicky, because he was farthest back, escaped. Snatching at the left hand basket, he pulled out a blue bottle and then drew in his head, arms and legs, so that when the rude and boisterous bandsmen approached to drag their captives into the city, the Red Jinn appeared to be nothing but a huge red jar. Thinking the jar must contain some mysterious treasure or jewels, the musicians lifted it carefully from Kabumpo's back and dispatched it by two drummers into the town. Randy had struck his head against a stone and lay perfectly senseless in the road. Tossing him carelessly into Jinnicky's seat, the bandsmen tied a rope around Kabumpo's trunk and began to pull and drag him up the hill. Had the Elegant Elephant not been dazed and half blinded by the trumpet blow, he might have resisted, but scarcely knowing what he was doing or where he was going, he plodded dully after his captors. As the procession passed through the city gates, Randy came to, and rubbing his eyes looked dizzly around him. And well he might, for the yellow city and its strange inhabitants were almost too ridiculous to believe.

"Am I seeing double, or what?" mumbled the boy, shaking his head, which still throbbed from the terrible fall.

"Double Up, and not What!" snapped the leader of the yellow band grimly. "This is Double Up, the famous city of the Doublemen." And doubling up his fists the bandmaster seemed daring Randy to dispute the matter. Randy, however, was too startled to speak again, for the bandmaster, his fellow musicians and all the people in Double Up, were two-faced. Imagine! They had no backs at all, so that no matter how they turned they were always facing him. It was dreadfully confusing when a Doubleman spoke, for both his faces talked at once and what one said the other contradicted, so there was no sense at all to the conversation.

"Knock the boy off the elephant!" shouted the bandmaster, with one face. "Take him to the King," advised the other, at which all the rest of the Doubles joined in and made such a racket that Randy could not discover what was to be done with him. He looked around anxiously for Jinnicky and seeing no sign of him tried to reach one of the Jinn's baskets. But as his fingers touched the handle the top jars and jugs cried out shrilly: "Master! Master!" and Randy, quivering with astonishment, drew back his hand. Fortunately the Doubles were making such a noise they did not hear the weird cries.

191

Crouching down among the cushions, wondering what in Oz had come over Kabumpo, who was moving along like a creature in a dream, Randy waited tensely for something to happen. As he had not been knocked off, he concluded they were taking him to the King, and in this he was right, for they were now passing along a broad avenue lined with a double row of yellow pear trees toward the tidy twin castles. Everything in Double Up was double, the houses were double, the windows and doors in the houses were double, the double-faced citizens walked stiffly in pairs and by the time Randy reached the double gates of the castle he was seeing everything double and was so giddy that he made no resistance whatever when he was rudely jerked off Kabumpo's back. But he did give a little scream of indignation as the Elegant Elephant was pushed, banged and driven through another double gateway. Why didn't Kabumpo turn around and trample on them? Randy himself, hustled roughly through the double doors of the castle, just could not understand it. Only the bandmaster accompanied him to the big double throne room. The Double King was sitting on his throne eating a pear, or rather two pears, and the bandmaster bowed first to one side of the King and then to the other. As he did so the King gave Randy a couple of mean looks.

"So you captured them?" muttered his Majesty's first face. "That elephant will be good for log rolling," observed his Majesty's second face. "I wonder to whom he belongs?"

"King, King, Double King, they'll never get him back again," chortled the bandmaster with one mouth. "The boy will make a good boot black," sneered the other. "This is his impairious Highness

King Too Too the Second, King, King, and Double King. Bow to your new sovereign." Jerking Randy by the arm and seeing that he was not going to bow, the bandmaster gave him a blow that sent him sprawling at the Double King's feet. It was all like some horrible nightmare and when Randy jumped up in a fury and threw himself upon his two-faced Majesty, he was soon overpowered by a Double Up guard and shaken into silence.

"Bring him to the dining hall while we dine, but give him nothing," commanded the Double King, with one mouth while he finished both pears with the other. "After dinner, we will break open that red jug." At these awful words and knowing they referred to Jinnicky, Randy pricked up his ears and as the Double King, followed by a double line of Double Courtiers, began to move slowly toward the dining hall, Randy tried desperately to think of some way to help himself and his luckless companions. The dining hall was long and elegant, with two beautifully set tables in the exact center. And Randy soon discovered why this was. Standing in a corner, watched over by the surly guard, the boy could not help feeling interested in the Double King's dinner. It took a long time, for the Doubles, having two mouths to feed, had to eat twice as much as an ordinary person. So, to begin with, they seated themselves at the first table and ate noisily and heartily; then, turning around, they seated themselves at the second table and gave the other side of their faces a chance.

"It must be pretty expensive to be a Double," reflected Randy, "and a great nuisance, too." On the whole he was glad he had only one face to wash, though eyes in the back of one's head would be handy things at times. Thanks to the magic dinner he had eaten with Jinnicky he was not bothered at all by the Double King's double feast. But he was tired of standing and felt a real relief when the King at last finished and started back to the throne room.

"Perhaps," thought Randy, as he was pulled along roughly by the Double Guard, "perhaps I'll think of some way to save Jinnicky when the time comes." But alas, he was to have no such opportunity. For no sooner had the King-King reached his throne than he cried out in a couple of very fierce voices.

"Take that boy to the dungeon and if he gives any trouble just chop off his head! Chop off his head!"

"Twice?" inquired the guard out of the corner of one of his mouths.

195

"Once!" shrieked the King at the top of both of his voices.

"But your Highness said once twice and twice once are twice," argued the guard stubbornly. Randy was so mixed up by this time that he could think of nothing to do or say at all and while the Doubles laughed and roared spitefully he was ignominiously dragged from the Double King's presence. The dungeon to which Randy was taken was exceedingly dark and dismal and as the double doors clanged shut and the double bolts shot into place, his heart sank to the bottom of his boots. How ever could he get out or find a way to help Jinnicky and Kabumpo. Two candles burned in a double candlestick on the rickety table, and flinging himself sadly on a heap of straw in the corner of the dungeon, Randy lay looking at their wavering flames, trying to plan some way to escape. But he was so worn out and weary from all the adventures and curious experiences of the day that, in spite of his discomfort and terrible anxiety, he soon fell into an uneasy and troubled slumber.

CHAPTER 15

Escape from Double Up

A LIGHT touch on the arm wakened Randy. The candles had burned out and it was quite dark in the dungeon.

"It's morning," whispered a cautious voice. "Come, take my hand and we'll soon be away from these double dealing dodos."

"Why, Jinnicky!" gasped the boy. "How did you ever find me? How can it be morning when it's so dark, and how are we to get past the guards?"

"Hold on to me and you'll soon see," chuckled Jinnicky in his jolly voice, and seizing Randy's arm hurried him out of the dungeon up a long flight of steps and finally into the great double kitchen of Too Too's castle. The light made Randy blink and dropping into the double cook's chair he took a long, deep breath. Sure enough, it was morning, and the fresh May breeze coming in through the double windows seemed perfectly delicious after the stifling air below. With a big sigh of relief Randy noted that Jinnicky's jar was not broken. Indeed, the Red Jinn looked shinier, saucier and more mischievous than ever.

"What happened?" begged Randy, as Jinnicky took off his red looking glasses and slipped them into his wide sleeve.

"Come and see, my mercy me!" With scarcely concealed merriment the little Jinn pattered toward Too Too's throne room. But even before they reached that spacious and elegant apartment, Randy saw the Double King's retainers doubled up in every direction, on the stairs, along the corridors and in every room and corner. Apparently they were fast asleep, and stepping softly, so as not to waken them, Randy hurried after Jinnicky. Not till he had seated himself on Too Too's throne did the Red Jinn reveal what had really taken place. Here, with his feet resting comfortably on the Double King's prostrate form, with fallen Doubles lying in heaps and mounds around them, Jinnicky began his story. The King and his subjects had passed nearly the whole night celebrating their victory over the travelers. Shut up in his jar Jinnicky had listened to long double speeches, double duets and the thunderous banging and tooting of the Doublemen's band. Toward morning Too Too, wearying of the clamor, decided to investigate the contents of the red jug.

"And then," murmured Jinnicky, leaning back with half closed eyes, "then I knew my turn had come. At the first touch on my lid I stuck up my head and so frightened Too Too that he fell over backwards, or rather frontwards, for he has, as you know, no back at all, and while his courtiers and musicians gaped with amazement I flung the contents of my blue bottle high into the air calling:

'Joonicky, Jonicky, Jornicky Junnicky!
Incense, blue incense, subdue everyoneicky.' "

"And it did, didn't it?" marveled Randy.
"Well, it certainly made them more sensible,"

agreed Jinnicky, looking around the throne room with quiet satisfaction. "Some people, my boy, are only sensible when they are insensible and while my blue incense still keeps them so, let us depart and shake the dust of this double dealing city from our doublets."

"But I don't see why you did not throw the incense when we first met them?" puzzled Randy, thinking of his uncomfortable night in the dungeon.

"Blue incense only works after three o'clock in the

morning," answered Jinnicky mysteriously. "That's why I had to wait, but as soon as it *did* take effect I put on my looking glasses and started to hunt you. It took me a long time to unbar that dungeon, but here you are and here I am. I suppose they did away with our fat friend?" he finished inquiringly.

Jinnicky tried to keep his voice indifferent and casual when he referred to Kabumpo, but Randy, with a little smile, saw the worried frown on his round little face.

"I believe he likes Kabumpo as much as I do," thought Randy, with a little sniff of satisfaction, and he quickly told the Jinn how the Elegant Elephant had been driven into the courtyard of the castle.

"Well," said Jinnicky, putting on his red glasses again, "in that case we might as well look around for the old gaboscis. He has all my magic, you know."

Rolling off the throne Jinnicky stepped carelessly over Too Too and, followed by Randy, marched resolutely from the yellow castle. The looking glasses led them to the meanest and smallest end of the courtyard. There they finally found Kabumpo, penned up in a log enclosure. Soon after he had been shut up the Elegant Elephant had recovered from the

201

trumpet blow and had thumped and bumped against the logs till he was black and blue and trumpeted till he was too hoarse to make another sound. Then, like Randy in his dungeon, he had given up and fallen into a heavy slumber. When the Red Jinn and the mountain boy reached the enclosure he was already

awake and banging and pushing furiously against the logs. Calling to him reassuringly, Randy after some difficulty, unbarred the door and the next minute the three adventurers were reunited.

Kabumpo had a huge lump between his eyes and the robe made from Nandywog's silk handkerchiefs was frayed and torn beyond recognition. He listened in a lofty and bored silence while the Red Jinn explained how he had overcome their enemies, thanked him gruffly for his trouble and suggested that they leave for other parts at once. This suited Randy and Jinnicky exactly and climbing thankfully aloft they begged him to start at once. So as not to waste any time Kabumpo put on the looking glasses and directing them to take him to Pumperdink, left the city of Double Up at a double quick pace, trumpeting with scorn as he swung through the double gates of the hateful city. Jinnicky, after peeping into both wicker baskets to make sure all his jugs and bottles were safe, settled back contentedly among his cushions.

"The thing to do," he concluded cheerfully, "is to profit by our mistakes. Now take that welcome band. That was quite an idea and took us completely by surprise. I'd expect horns on a wild animal to be dangerous, but horns in a band, never. We looked for music and instead received blows. Altogether a noteworthy victory for the enemy, which we might sum up by saying: 'Lively blows were struck by the enemy and as the invaders could not beat their band they were forthwith taken and dragged into the city.'

203

"For who'd expect a sliding flute
To up and rap you on the snoot?"

Jinnicky looked so comical chanting his ridiculous verses that Randy burst out laughing, but Kabumpo was still mad.

"Stop it! Stop it," he shouted violently, "or I'll take off these glasses and not go another step." The lump on his forehead was the only reminder he wanted of their wretched encounter with the double band. He could not yet understand how the fellows had got the best of him and the poor figure he had cut in the affair made him feel perfectly savage.

"Notwithstanding and nevertheless," continued Jinnicky in a low voice to Randy, "I've a mind to equip my army with shooting horns, disguise them as musicians and outwit all my enemies."

"Have you any of that blue incense left?" asked Randy, after agreeing that Jinnicky's idea might be a good thing. The incense seemed a handy weapon on a journey as perilous as this.

"Plenty," smiled the Red Jinn, nodding his head gaily. "In those baskets, my lad, I believe I have a cure for any emergency."

"Do you have anything to keep you from talking all the time?" snapped Kabumpo disagreeably.

"Even that! Even that, my dear El!" Imperturbed, Jinnicky drew out his silver bell and rang it briskly three times. "Nothing like food for keeping a body from talking," he observed slyly, as the turbaned slave set down appetizing trays before him

and Randy. "Bacon, eggs, waffles and honey. My mercy me! What a treat!"

"Shut up!" rumbled Kabumpo, pounding sullenly down the hill. And while Randy and Jinnicky breakfasted heartily from the magic trays, the Elegant

Elephant snatched savage bites from the trees and bushes. But as the morning wore on Kabumpo's ill temper wore off. They had soon reached the foot of the hill and following the tug of the Jinn's glasses the Elegant Elephant was making his way through a small, pleasant wood. The trees were just far enough apart for comfort and the air was so fragrant and delicious that Kabumpo began to forget his unpleasant experiences in Double Up.

"We should reach the Gilliken Country any minute now," he called back to Randy. "There's the Winkie River just ahead and that will bring us quite near the border."

"Say, won't Kettywig be surprised when we march into the castle?" exulted Randy, standing up to get a glimpse of the river. "And won't Faleero be furious? Are you sure you can restore the King and the others, Jinnicky?"

"Reasonably so, reasonably so," murmured the Red Jinn, shaking his head like a little china mandarin, and he proceeded to give Randy a lively lecture on red magic, its causes and principal effects. While they were talking Kabumpo had stepped out of the wood and seeing a broad, tumbling river before them, Jinnicky hurriedly crawled past Randy and snatched the looking glasses off Kabumpo's trunk.

"No use swimming so early in the day," smiled Jinnicky, holding on to Kabumpo's ear to steady himself.

"That's so!" puffed Kabumpo, coming to a stop on the brink of the river. "I expect those specs would have pulled me in, ears over hind quarters. But if I don't swim, how are we to get across?" Jinnicky, handing the looking glasses to Randy, began rummaging in the left hand wicker basket. Bringing up a green flower pot containing a small plant, he flung it carelessly over Kabumpo's head. The flower pot, striking on a stone, broke into a hundred fragments and while Kabumpo and Randy looked on in amazement a tremendous green spruce sprang up, growing like a magic bean stalk before their eyes. Randy was wondering what good a tree would do them, when the spruce, as if cut down by a mighty and invisible ax, fell crashing across the stream.

"There you are! There you are!" Snapping his fingers joyfully Randy crawled back to his seat and Kabumpo, with a snort of approval, stepped out on the trunk. In spite of his huge size and great weight, Kabumpo was sure-footed and fearless and without

KABUMPO WAS SURE-FOOTED AND FEARLESS

208

mishap or misstep crossed the river safely on the magic bridge.

"A tree-mendously successful idea," chuckled the Jinn, handing Kabumpo the red looking glasses:

"The river's behind us, the broad plain before;
To-morrow will find us at Pumperdink's door."

"What else have you in those baskets?" asked Randy curiously.

"Well, here's a cooky jar that's always full and a water pitcher that's never empty," answered Jinnicky, diving into the right hand basket, "so let us refresh ourselves. How about a cooky, El? How about a cooky?" Jinnicky wagged his finger roguishly at Kabumpo, who was looking over his shoulder to see what the Jinn had taken out of his baskets.

"One cooky is about as much good to an elephant as one bullet to an army," sniffed Kabumpo scornfully.

"But wait—" laughed the Jinn, and hurrying out on Kabumpo's head, he tilted the cooky jar so that a perfect cascade of crisp, toothsome wafers poured down the elephant's trunk. Now if there was one thing Kabumpo liked better than peanuts it was cookies and while he tossed down dozen after dozen, Jinnicky and Randy refreshed themselves from the black pitcher and ate a heap of the cookies themselves. Kabumpo, after downing two hundred and fifty, quenched his thirst in the Winkie River, adjusted the red looking glasses and once more turned his face toward the west. To tell the truth, he was

homesick for a sight of the castle and his own quiet and comfortable quarters. He missed his white marble bath and his hundred and ten robes and cloaks of silk and velvet. Traveling was all very well, but for the present, Kabumpo had had quite enough of it. So the Red Jinn's looking glasses, fast as they drew him along, could not go too fast for the Elegant Elephant. And when, about three o'clock, he stepped from the yellow country into the purple dominions of the Gillikens, he gave a long low whistle of relief and satisfaction.

CHAPTER 16

Meanwhile, in Pumperdink

NOW, while Kabumpo and Randy had been traveling rapidly in three directions to help them, the Pumperdinkians, under the rule of Faleero and Kettywig were having a blue and dismal time of it. Soon after the wedding, which had been celebrated with great haste and magnificence, Faleero's vindictive and spiteful nature began to assert itself. Too old, stiff and crotchety to enjoy any fun or pleasure herself, she immediately passed laws against all kinds of amusement. No singing, music or dancing was permitted in Pumperdink. Games were strictly forbidden; even the children's hoops, marbles and balls were confiscated by the guards and two small boys caught flying kites in the courtyard were dipped three times in the purple well.

Everybody was dipped sooner or later and the chains operating the huge well bucket clanked dismally all day long. Grandfathers and uncles who craved a little relaxation had to retire to their cellars for a quiet game of checkers or chess. Everything was against the law and the law was against everything. Any one caught laughing on the King's Highway was thrown into prison for a week and with sad, dolorous faces the usually gay and carefree citizens tip-toed cautiously about their business. Kettywig, who had meant to rule the kingdom himself and lead a life of ease and jollity, bitterly regretted his bargain with the wicked old fairy. Faleero would allow him to have nothing to say about affairs of state and bullied, scolded and cuffed him from morning till night. She took away his pipe and fed him on oatmeal and weak tea, her own favorite diet, and when Kettywig timidly suggested that they have roast beef and ice cream on Wednesdays, she flew into a passion and had him locked securely in the tower.

Faleero had never really cared for Kettywig and with him so conveniently put out of the way she proceeded to govern Pumperdink as she pleased. Closely attended by her three ancient ladies in waiting, she stamped furiously about the palace giving her ill-natured commands and terrifying courtiers and servants alike. No one dared to defy the false Queen, for on her first day in the palace she had turned the cook to a cocoanut and had him baked in a pie. Fearful of her temper and her magic, the poor Pumperdinkians kept out of Faleero's way whenever possible and longed heartily for the old happy days under King Pompus and Queen Pozy Pink.

The disappearance of the Elegant Elephant was the only ray of cheer in all those gloomy times. Each loyal subject of the old King felt that Kabumpo had gone for help and would some day return to save them. Every night the guardsmen gathered in a distant corner of the royal gardens and tried to devise some way to seize and subdue their terrible Queen. But at the slightest sign of insurrection Faleero resorted to magic and after four of the guards had

FALEERO STAMPED FURIOUSLY ABOUT THE PALACE

215

been turned to stone, the others sadly gave up the attempt.

All but General Quakes. Indignation and fury burned in his tempery but honest breast and one night, after all his comrades had retired, he put on his best uniform, buckled on his largest sword and marched determinedly out of the city. Taking much the same direction Kabumpo had traveled, he set his face toward the Emerald City, determined to seek and obtain aid from Ozma herself. By some good fortune he skirted the River Road that had carried the Elegant Elephant so far out of his way and without any serious mishaps or encounters, reached the capital in safety—but only to discover that Ozma, the Wizard of Oz and the most famous and important of her advisers had gone to the castle of Glinda the Good Sorceress, who was celebrating her hundredth anniversary as Ruler of the South. And while the servants in the castle and the citizens themselves showed General Quakes every courtesy and listened with great sympathy to his story of the disasters in Pumperdink, they could do nothing at all to help him.

So there was nothing for the General to do but march on to the south. He was dreadfully tired and footsore, but it took more than that to discourage this doughty patriot and after resting one night in Ozma's palace, he borrowed a tremendous pair of boots from the Soldier with Green Whiskers—his own being perfectly worn out—and set boldly out for Glinda's Red Castle.

CHAPTER 17

Ozwoz the Wonderful

ONCE he had crossed into his own country, Kabumpo cheered up tremendously. Had he not successfully carried out his plans for saving the kingdom? On his back rode the famous Red Jinn of Ev, whose magic was ten times more powerful than the magic of Faleero. Before another day passed, Pumperdink would be restored to its rightful rulers and he, the Elegant Elephant of Oz, fittingly rewarded for his enterprise and bravery in bringing about the disenchantment of its sovereigns. He would put in a few good words for Randy, too, for surely the boy had proved himself on this journey. He would engage another attendant and Randy should henceforth be his friend and companion, free to go and come as he wished. Looking back at the handsome young mountaineer, Kabumpo gave him an affectionate wink and breaking into an old Gilliken ballad, sung, it must be confessed, through his trunk, swung cheerfully along the purple highway.

Jinnicky had retired into his jar for his afternoon nap, and Randy, resting comfortably against Jinnicky's wicker seat, was speculating upon the further contents of the wizard's baskets. He was not paying much attention to the scenery and when Kabumpo, with a snort of displeasure, suddenly snatched off Jinnicky's red looking glasses, Randy leaped anxiously to his feet to see what had happened. Nothing, he discovered, had happened yet, but from what he saw, something was about to happen, something highly unpleasant and disastrous. The highway, cutting through a small wood, had come out and quite suddenly ended on the edge of a broad plain. Marching in level rows across the plain came an army of stiff and enormous soldiers each standing twice as high as an ordinary Oz man.

"Jinnicky! Jinnicky! Wake up!" Pounding on Jinnicky's jar with the handle of his sword, Randy looked wildly over his shoulder. Kabumpo, thrusting the looking glasses in his pocket, snatched up a tree by the roots and trumpeting like a steamboat whistle, prepared to defend himself. Wakened by Randy's taps and Kabumpo's furious snorting, Jinnicky stuck up his head. His sleepy eyes snapped wide open at sight of the advancing foe.

"My mercy me!" puffed the little Jinn, bounding out of his seat and grabbing the handle of his left hand basket. "Another war? So soon? These military receptions are making me nervous, preserve us." Fumbling in the basket as he talked, Jinnicky dragged out his blue bottle, and though there was still quite a distance between, uncorked the incense and hurled it into the midst of the marching men. "Lucky this works in the daytime," he panted, catching hold of Randy to steady himself.

"But it isn't!" shrilled Randy, clutching Jinnicky firmly around the waist. "They're still coming, they're aiming their guns. Great Gillikens, they're going to fire!" Dropping on his stomach, Randy pulled Jinnicky down beside him, and rolling over and over till he could reach his right hand basket, the Red Jinn pulled out a large blue vase and tossed it high into the air. The soldiers, squinting sternly along their gun barrels, were now so close that Randy could count the wooden buttons on their uniforms. But just as the guns with a thousand deafening bangs went off, the blue vase, expanding to enormous dimensions, swooped down over Kabumpo and his companions, covering and enclosing them completely. Bullets pattered like hail stones on the sides of their strange refuge and peering through the milky blue glass, Randy saw the soldiers charging in waves and columns and piling up in heaps around the base.

"How long will this jug hold together?" wheezed Kabumpo, pressing his trunk against the sides. "You know, there's something extremely funny about this army, fellows, something strange, odd, not to say peculiar."

"I agree with you," muttered Jinnicky, wiping off his red face with a bright silk handkerchief. "They are not real soldiers, or my blue incense would have rendered them insensible. A fortunate thing I had my expanding vase along. Otherwise we should have been shot and trampled to blotting paper."

"Not before I'd mowed down a few rows," sniffed the Elegant Elephant a bit resentfully. "What was the big hurry anyway?"

"You can't argue with bullets, my dear El." Jinnicky spoke kindly but firmly. "And here we will stay till they disperse, retreat and march back where they came from."

"They're beginning to move off now," volunteered Randy, who had slid to the ground and was looking intently through the glass. "All but the ones who have fallen."

"Well, why don't they pick themselves up?" scoffed Kabumpo. "Nobody shot them."

"Because—they are wood!" announced Randy, after a long, incredulous stare. "I can see them quite plainly now and they're nothing but wooden soldiers, Kabumpo."

"Well, wouldn't that curl your hair?" Pressing closer to the side of the vase, Kabumpo snapped his little eyes inquisitively at the retreating army and their fallen comrades heaped around the base of the curious stronghold.

"My mercy me!" puffed Jinnicky, taking out a small red note book and making excited entries and notes. "My mercy me! A mechanical army, as I live!

I'm getting lots of ideas on this journey, lads, and a mechanical army is the best of them all. Conquer your enemies without loss or inconvenience and when the troopers wear out their coats and uniforms, just give them a coat and trousers of paint. Clever, that. Eh, Randy?"

"Wonder who owns them," mused the boy, rubbing his sleeve against the glass so he could see better. "Look, here comes somebody now!" Stepping briskly across the plain was a tall, exceedingly fine looking fellow in a dashing, wide-brimmed hat and long, sweeping cape. As he came nearer he seemed very much shocked and surprised at the enormous vase and its occupants. At a safe distance he viewed it from all sides.

"Heave up this jug and I'll shake some sense into the impudent rascal," rumbled Kabumpo, beginning to swing his trunk angrily. But Jinnicky had a better plan. Climbing down the ladder he broke a large hole in the vase with his red umbrella. Tying a white handkerchief to the end of the umbrella, he thrust it through the opening and waited with scarcely concealed impatience for the enemy to approach. This the enemy did quite cheerfully, tramping unconcernedly over his fallen soldiers. For a

THE STRANGER WAS THE FIRST TO SPEAK

224

long minute the stranger and the Red Jinn regarded one another but the stranger was the first to speak.

"I am Ozwoz, the Wonderful," he announced in a pompous voice. "Who are you?"

"I am the Red Jinn of Ev," answered Jinnicky, with dignity.

"Im—agine!" drawled Ozwoz, stepping back to have a better look.

> "Imagine away, if you must, but take care;
> A Jinn who's insulted is dangerous. Beware!"

"Well, thanks for warning me," yawned Ozwoz, pushing back his plumed hat in a bored fashion. "I intended to have my army destroy you utterly, but since they have failed, let's forget it and talk about something else."

"Your manners are atrocious, sir!" Kabumpo, unable to contain himself any longer, glared at the cloaked figure. "How dare you try to annihilate innocent travelers?"

"Oh, are you innocent travelers?" Ozwoz glanced curiously through the side of the vase at Kabumpo and Randy, and Randy, crowding close to the Red Jinn, spoke up boldly.

"Are you a wizard?" he asked sternly. "If you are,

225

you're breaking the law and you well know it. The practice of magic is forbidden in Oz."

"Aha—but I am a wozard!" answered Ozwoz, with a superior smile. "And nothing has been said about wozardry in the laws of the country. But come, let

us cease this useless chatter. Since I have failed to capture you, let me captivate you. As a host you will find me amusing and gay and since night draws on, perhaps you will honor me with your company in my castle.

"Don't do it," warned Kabumpo in a hoarse whisper. "I wouldn't trust him as far as I could fling a ton of gold bricks." Jinnicky, rubbing his chin thoughtfully, considered the wozard's invitation.

"Oh, come on, let's go," begged Randy, who was burning up with curiosity to know how Ozwoz operated his mechanical army. "I don't believe he'll try any more tricks. Besides, Jinnicky has plenty of magic himself." Ozwoz had walked off a few paces and stood gazing indifferently at the skyline while the three travelers made up their minds. When Jinnicky, after a little argument with Kabumpo, called out that they would be pleased to accept his kind invitation, the wozard nodded amiably. Taking out a small metal instrument, he clicked it seven times. Instantly the soldiers who had fallen rose up and at another set of signals from the wozard, faced about and started to march stiffly toward a small park ahead. Unhurriedly Ozwoz stalked behind them. Then Jinnicky, tapping the vase with his umbrella, dissolved the glass into smoke. He and Randy mounted the elephant and Kabumpo, very stiff and disapproving, followed the wozard to his Castle.

It was a small, cozy castle set in the center of a neat park. Beside the castle stood a huge wooden

227

armory and into this the wooden soldiers solemnly marched themselves. Their comrades were already in and ranged in rigid rows in the huge barracks. Taking their proper places in the ranks the newcomers, after marking time for a few seconds, ceased all motion and Ozwoz calmly locked them up for the night. There were two thousand of the wooden warriors and Jinnicky could scarcely conceal his envy.

Ozwoz, now that he had given up all idea of destroying them, proved extremely likeable and friendly and did everything in his power to amuse them. While the wozard and Jinnicky discussed magic and sorcery, Kabumpo and Randy had a swim in the private pool of the palace. Then, greatly refreshed and as hungry as bears, they joined the two necromancers in the spacious dining hall. The wozard's servants were noiseless and invisible and served the dinner with such skill and dispatch that Kabumpo could not help feeling a grudging admiration for their master. They had thoughtfully supplied him with crushed raw vegetables and hay and he enjoyed his dinner quite as much as Randy and Jinnicky enjoyed the roast chicken and candied vegetables, strawberries and Ozade. Altogether it was a gay and memorable evening.

After dinner Jinnicky did some magic transformations. These Ozwoz followed with some amazing tricks of his own and finally, after much arguing and coaxing, agreed to trade one of his wooden soldiers for the cooky jar that never was empty. When the great fellow, in answer to the wozard's summons, tramped stolidly into their presence, Randy could hardly contain himself. Ozwoz carefully explained how he worked. All his troopers, he told them, were named John and numbered from one to two thousand.

"Then I hope you have given us a low number," laughed Jinnicky, "for how would it be to call 'Forward march, John One Thousand Nine Hundred and Ninety-Nine?'" Ozwoz smiled at this and confessed that the soldier's name was John-one or Johnwan. The name, Randy decided, suited him very well. Johnwan's face was round and pleasant with a small brown painted moustache. His uniform was purple and white with twenty wooden buttons on the trousers and coat. A tall shako hat of white fur and real purple leather boots lent him dignity and importance. He carried his rifle, a magic, self-loading and cleaning affair, with careless assurance and grace and at a double click from the wozard, smartly saluted his new owners. Johnwan could obey seven commands. At one click of the starter he marched forward, at two, he faced about and marched in the opposite direction. At three, Johnwan halted, at four he fired off his gun, at five, he seized the enemy in his arms and held him till wanted. At six, he dropped his captive and at seven picked himself up if he had fallen. Even Kabumpo felt that the Red Jinn had made a good trade. He longed for the moment when he would march into Pumperdink with the giant wooden soldier tramping beside him.

The swim and excellent supper had put the Elegant Elephant in a high good humor and before long he was telling Ozwoz the whole curious story of their adventures, for by this time they had entirely forgiven and almost forgotten the wozard's attempt to destroy them. Ozwoz was deeply interested in the King's enchantment and after referring to his maps told Kabumpo they were but three hills and a forest from their goal.

After Jinnicky had sung a number of songs at his own request, after Kabumpo had rendered a few selections on the wozard's gold harp and Randy had showed Ozwoz the Gilliken clod and hop, they all retired and slept soundly and well till morning. Then, having eaten a hearty breakfast they bade Ozwoz

THE RED JINN TRADED HIS COOKY JAR FOR JOHNWAN

231

a regretful farewell and in good spirits set out for Pumperdink. For a long time the wozard watched them marching across the purple plain. Then, as he had some new magic experiments to perfect, and wished to practice using his new cooky jar, he went into his castle and closed the door.

CHAPTER 18

The Elegant Elephant Uses His Head

SO as not to waste any time, or take any wrong
turnings, Kabumpo had again donned the Jinn's
red looking glasses. Jinnicky rode high and comfortably on his wicker seat; Randy, perched on Kabumpo's head held the metal controller that guided
the action of Johnwan the soldier. Johnwan marched
precisely and well, stepping so high that he seldom
tripped and as he never talked back, argued or made

233

foolish suggestions, he was an excellent addition to the party. Indeed, the Red Jinn was so delighted with Johnwan that he planned to build a wooden army of his own when he returned to Ev.

"Then you may have Johnwan for a bodyguard," he promised generously, "but first I must use him for a model."

"Well, he certainly is a model soldier," chuckled Kabumpo, staring approvingly at the huge wooden figure tramping along just ahead of him. "He may be mighty useful when we reach Pumperdink."

"By the way, have you planned any course of action when we do reach there?" inquired Jinnicky, noting with satisfaction that they had put one hill behind them. "Before I restore the Royal Family I must find the vanishing point, in other words, the exact spot on which each of them disappeared. My famous yellow incense will then do the rest, but we must be careful not to fall into Faleero's clutches or get ourselves captured or enchanted."

"Is the blue incense all gone?" asked Randy, looking rather worried.

"Every grain," answered Jinnicky, "and it's too bad, for that would have overcome Faleero and the whole population and given us plenty of time to work out our magic. My mercy me! How these hill roads do joggle one. There goes Johnwan over a tree stump." Randy hastily clicked the controller, brought the wooden soldier to his feet and headed him in the right direction, as Kabumpo thoughtfully mounted the second hill. He was not sure himself just what he would do when they reached Pumperdink. Perhaps if they rushed pell mell into the royal city and took Faleero by surprise, Jinnicky could work his magic before the old fury had time to try any witchwork, so, when Jinnicky asked him again what he planned to do, he merely flapped his great ears and informed him solemnly that he intended to use his head.

"Very good," approved Jinnicky, clasping his hands over his middle. "Use your head by all means. It's big enough to serve all four of us. In fact, I never saw a more long-headed creature in my life:

> "Long-headed, hee, hee!
> And three hearty ho, ho's!
> It's three yards from his eyes
> To the tip of his nose."

"This is no time for joking," said Kabumpo, looking back severely at Jinnicky. "Besides, people in glass houses shouldn't throw stones."

"That's so," agreed the Jinn quite amiably. "Are you referring to my glass palace or my jar?"

"Oh, look!" put in Randy, anxious to change the subject before his two best friends got into a serious quarrel. "We can see the towers of Pumperdink's castle from here. Only one hill and a forest to go now!" Taking off the looking glasses long enough to assure himself that the towers showing above the tree tops were really those of the King's palace, Kabumpo with a long sigh of satisfaction clapped them on again and headed recklessly down the hill. The rest of the journey took barely an hour. The forest was the most difficult, for Johnwan kept bumping into trees. Randy found that if he walked beside the wooden warrior he could guide him easily around them, though he had to run to keep up with Johnwan's long strides. But fortunately the forest was small and when at last they stepped out they found themselves on the King's Highway that led directly into Pumperdink. It was a little after noon, and Randy rather nervously wished Kabumpo and Johnwan were not so big and conspicuous.

"Maybe we'd better wait till night," suggested the boy, mounting Jinnicky's ladder and seating himself on Kabumpo's head. But Kabumpo shook his head.

"The people of Pumperdink will know I have come to help them," he stated calmly. "When they get a glimpse of Johnwan and our friend yonder," Kabumpo swung his trunk carelessly in Jinnicky's direction, "they will fall in behind us and by the time we reach the palace we'll have a regular army of rebellion."

Kabumpo was right. No sooner had they entered the gates of the city than the Pumperdinkians gathered around them in huge crowds, and throwing fear and discretion to the winds, shouted their welcome at the top of their voices. Those in their houses, looking out to see what the commotion was about, hastily joined the others and seizing sticks, brooms, spades and umbrellas, ran joyfully after Kabumpo and Johnwan. Most of them were a dark purple from frequent dippings in the royal well, but Kabumpo and Randy, Johnwan and Jinnicky put new courage and confidence into Pompus' downtrodden and sorely abused subjects. Yelling threats and defiance they proceeded boldly to the palace. The guards, brandishing their pikes, fell in step with Johnwan and by the time Faleero, followed by her three old ladies in waiting, heard the deafening uproar and rushed out to see what was the matter, the rebels were al-

JOHNWAN GRASPED FALEERO AND MARCHED ON

238

ready mounting the steps of the imperial palace. Faleero, astonished by the unexpected appearance of Kabumpo and the giant soldier and the extreme suddenness of the uprising, gave a howl of anger and in high, indignant screeches ordered the crowd to disperse.

Randy, closely watching Johnwan mount the steps, made ready to halt the giant soldier the minute they reached the top. But as Johnwan, closely followed by Kabumpo, stepped up on the broad flagged terrace before the palace door, Faleero flung up her arms and hissed three shrill magic incantations. Kabumpo, in the act of snatching the old fury, was halted so abruptly that he turned a complete somersault, hurling Randy and Jinnicky to the ground. Randy, shocked by the fall and without intending in the least to do so, clicked Johnwan's controller five times and the wozard's wooden soldier, whom magic could not stop or injure, obeying the order to seize the enemy, grasped Faleero in his wooden arms, marched straight through the front door of the palace and out of the back, on and on, tramping steadily and calmly through the park, the fields beyond and finally disappearing over a purple hilltop.

As soon as Johnwan had seized Faleero the whole

239

company, which had been halted by her magic, found themselves able to move again. Kabumpo, who was quite ridiculously standing on his head, quickly assumed a more usual and dignified position. Randy, not realizing that he had given Johnwan the signal to seize the enemy, now jumped up and ran wildly after him.

"Stop! Come back! Johnwan! Johnwan!" he called frantically. But Johnwan was already far away and could neither hear nor obey him. Suddenly remembering the metal controller, Randy rushed back to look for it. But when he was flung from Kabumpo's back it had rolled out of his hand and though he searched and searched he could find no trace of it. The Pumperdinkians, overjoyed at the disappearance of the evil old Queen were hugging one another, dancing jigs and in vociferous shouts and songs expressing their satisfaction and approval. Jinnicky, who had landed flat on his nose in the palace doorway, now rolled over and as Randy came hurrying breathlessly toward him pulled himself up by the gold door jamb.

"My mercy me!" he spluttered, looking reproachfully at Kabumpo. "I'm cracked, jarred and positively jellied. You told me you intended to use your head, old Gaboscis, but I never expected you to stand on it. My mercy me! Travel is very broadening, very broadening indeed!" He rubbed his nose tenderly, for it had suffered a complete flattening. "Where is that old woman and what happened?"

"Johnwan has her!" panted Randy. "And he's marching on and on and dear knows where to. I've lost the metal signal and we'll never see him again."

"You must have given him the command to seize the enemy when you fell," wheezed Kabumpo,

241

straightening his jeweled headpiece. "And a grumpy good thing, too."

"But who's to stop Johnwan and what will become of him?" wailed Randy, staring disconsolately at the Jinn. "Will he just march on till he falls into the sea or is burned up on the Deadly Desert?"

"I suppose so," sighed Jinnicky, taking off his lid and scratching his red head sorrowfully, "and it's a mean shame, for now I shall have no mechanical army. But never mind. He has served us faithfully and well in carrying off Faleero, for remember, wherever he goes, she goes too. Do speak to your countrymen, El, old fellow. Tell them if they return quietly to their homes I will restore their rightful sovereigns as soon or sooner than possible." This Kabumpo was only too glad to do, and with repeated bows to the Red Jinn and resounding cheers the crowd began to move off, and, much relieved, the rescue party hurried into the palace. The servants and courtiers had seen Faleero carried off by the giant soldier and knowing they had nothing to fear gave Kabumpo and his friends a rousing welcome and did everything they could to help with the disenchantment. Going immediately to the royal dining hall, Kabumpo had footmen place chairs in the exact places where the King, Queen, Prince Pompa, Princess Peg Amy and the little Princess had sat at the ill-fated dinner. Finding the exact spot on which the Prime Pumper had stood was more difficult. But as Kabumpo remarked to Randy, the old goose had so little wit and was of so little importance, it would be no great matter if he stayed out of sight forever.

The Red Jinn had now taken out his bottle of yellow incense and after sprinkling a few grains on each chair and the approximate spot where Pumper had stood, began whirling round and round like a top, mumbling an indistinguishable jargon of magic words and sentences. Randy was so interested that he almost forgot to breathe and Kabumpo, his ears fairly quivering with suspense and excitement, kept his eyes glued on the empty chairs. The servants and courtiers had been sent from the room, but through the curtains and cracks in the doors they peered with eager interest and curiosity. After whirling for three full minutes, Jinnicky came to a standstill, calling in a loud imperious voice:

"I do now command you to reappear, most Royal Rulers and Imperial Family of Pumperdink. Reappear, do you hear!" Taking off his lid, Jinnicky stared intently at the golden chairs. But to his furious consternation, to Randy's and Kabumpo's deep disappointment, nothing happened at all. After staring at the chairs so hard that their eyes began to water, the three friends looked anxiously at one another.

"Great Grump! Is your powder wet? Have you forgotten your magic, or what?" choked Kabumpo, almost ready to cry with vexation.

"Neither!" Jinnicky flopped disconsolately down on the King's footstool. "They have not vanished, after all. They have been transformed."

"Transformed?" exploded Kabumpo wrathfully. "Well, untransform them!"

"But first we must discover to what they have been changed," said Jinnicky, a bit stiffly. "Say, where's that other rascal? Fetch in that false King. Where's Kettywig?" Running to the kitchen door, Jinnicky banged it open so violently that the cook and four footmen who were taking turns at the keyhole fell headlong into the room.

"Yes! Yes! Yes! Yes!" mumbled the servants, bouncing up like balls and disappearing in four different directions. But when Kettywig was brought from the tower he could tell them nothing. In piteous tones he explained how he had been half starved

THE RED JINN BEGAN WHIRLING ROUND AND ROUND LIKE A TOP

and locked up by the wicked old fairy. Faleero had planned everything and he knew nothing at all about magic or transformations, and heartily wished himself back in his quiet village.

"Humph!" sniffed Jinnicky contemptuously. "A fine looking ruler you are, with all those bumps and scratches. Take away this hand-decorated King, and when we settle more important matters we'll deal with him as he deserves." Randy felt a little sorry for the forlorn and hungry looking fellow. He felt that Kettywig had already been punished enough, but thinking it best not to interfere, he said nothing. There were, as Jinnicky had said, so many more important matters to be cleared up. He sighed as he thought of Johnwan tramping on and on through deserts and over mountains. Even now his handsome soldier might be crumpled up at the bottom of some gorge or ravine or stuck in the mud of some deep mountain lake. Johnwan was to have belonged to him some day and he hated to have him broken or destroyed. So he sighed again as he looked inquiringly at Kabumpo and Jinnicky.

The Jinn had taken down both wicker baskets and was rummaging first in one and then in the other. He had just brought out a tube-like red bottle when the castle bell pealed noisily. Randy, rushing after the footman who opened the door, saw six people standing on the step. A dark-haired Princess wearing a tall, emerald-studded crown, a little girl, a fellow with a pumpkin head, a funny, bald-headed old gentleman, a scarecrow and General Quakes.

"Why, it's Ozma!" gulped Kabumpo, who was right in back of Randy, "and the Wizard of Oz! Dorothy, my dear, how are you? And the Scarecrow, as I live! Now everything will be fine! Jinnicky, Jinnick—y! Here's the Wizard!" While Kabumpo in flowery phrases and with wide gestures continued to welcome the celebrities, Randy dashed back to the Red Jinn. He found Jinnicky sitting glumly on the King's footstool.

"Now everything's ruined," he groaned, rolling his glass eyes tragically at the boy. "Why does that meddling Wizard have to come fooling around just as I'm beginning to get *my* magic working? Now he'll take all the credit and I might just as well have stayed at home." Randy could not help sympathizing with him. He, too, would have liked to see Jinnicky restore Pumperdink's sovereigns without any help. Suddenly a splendid idea popped into his head.

247

"Come on!" he whispered mysteriously. "Come on, before they see us." Taking a wicker basket in each hand he ran out into the kitchen, through the kitchen door and on into the castle garden, the little Jinn pattering inquiringly behind him.

CHAPTER 19

More Mysteries

GENERAL QUAKES, as you have probably
guessed, had finally reached Glinda's palace in
the Quadling country. Pouring out the story of
Pumperdink's misfortune he begged Ozma to return
with him and save his unhappy country from
Faleero. This Ozma had immediately agreed to do,
bringing Dorothy, the Wizard of Oz, the Scarecrow,
and Jack Pumpkinhead along. They had come on

one of the Wizard's wishing pills, and being wished a place is much, much simpler than traveling by the usual methods. Indeed, five minutes after General Quakes had arrived at Glinda's, Ozma and her councillors were standing on the steps of Pompus' purple palace.

Dorothy, a little mortal girl from Kansas who lives with Ozma in the Emerald City and who has been in several adventures with Kabumpo, begged him to lead them at once to the scene of the disappearance. The Scarecrow, that amiable, straw-stuffed gentleman, knew him too, and while Kabumpo had a sly habit of snatching wisps of straw from his person, he was, notwithstanding, quite fond of the elegant old pachyderm. As they all hurried along the corridor, Kabumpo told them of his journey to the Red Jinn's castle and of the soothsayer's prediction that only the Red Jinn could help restore the vanished ones. Then he explained how Johnwan had carried off Faleero and all that had happened after their arrival in Pumperdink.

"Then we're too late," exclaimed the little Wizard, looking terribly annoyed. "If this Red Jinn is as powerful as you say, he has probably solved the whole mystery by this time." Wagging his head sadly Kabumpo described the failure of Jinnicky's yellow incense, at which the Wizard cheered up immediately. If he succeeded where the Red Jinn had failed, it would be a real feather in his cap. Feeling that his reputation as Wizard of Oz was at stake, he almost trod on Kabumpo's heels in his anxiety to reach the scene of action. Transformations were right in his line and he felt sure that in his famous black bag there was magic enough to undo all of Faleero's spells and enchantments. Ozma was a fairy, herself, so quite confidently they entered the dining hall of the castle to restore King Pompus to his throne. Kabumpo was surprised not to find Randy and the Red Jinn, and apologetically explained that they must have stepped out for a minute. Dorothy and Ozma were eager to meet the famous little wizard of Ev for Jack Pumpkinhead had given them glowing descriptions of the Red Jinn's red glass palace, and his magic dinner bell was now one of the important treasures of Oz. But the Wizard of Oz was secretly delighted. In the absence of Jinnicky he hoped to restore the royal family himself. Opening his black bag he began carefully laying out his magic powders, bottles and instruments.

Meanwhile, Jinnicky and Randy had reached the

251

end of the garden and leaning breathlessly against the hedge, Randy disclosed his plan.

"All you have to do is to put on your looking glasses and ask them to take us to the King," whispered the boy. "Whatever made us forget?"

"My mercy me! The very thing! The very thing!" Kabumpo had returned Jinnicky's specs soon after Faleero had been carried off by Johnwan. Taking them from his sleeve the Red Jinn put them on and started to run as fast as his little legs would carry him through Pompus' private park. Randy, seeing a small donkey tied to a tree and thinking the glasses might take them a long way, untied the small creature and ran after Jinnicky. Fortunately the donkey was strong and gentle and helping the little Jinn to his back, Randy mounted up behind. With a resigned sigh Jinnicky transferred his glasses to the donkey's nose and away went the little animal at break-neck speed straight into Follensby Forest. With his arms clasped around the donkey's neck, expecting to fly over its ears any minute, Jinnicky blinked, groaned and shuddered while Randy, weighed down by the wicker baskets, had all he could do to keep his seat. Both had imagined the victims of Faleero's magic would be quite near the castle and noted with growing alarm that the donkey was carrying them deeper and deeper into Follensby Forest.

When, after an hour or so, he pushed his way through a cluster of vines and bushes, galloped across a small clearing and straight into Faleero's shabby hut, Randy gave a scream of surprise. Trotting over to the fireplace, the donkey lifted his head, brayed six times and came to a complete standstill. Then closing his eyes and dropping one hip he seemed to lose all interest in the affair. The fireplace was simply enormous, taking up the whole side of the cabin and making the little room look smaller even than it was. Recovering his specs, Jinnicky slid to the floor and poked his head inquiringly up the chimney.

"Do you suppose they are up there?" he puffed, as Randy jumped down and set the wicker baskets on a chair. The windows were so small and dirty that it was quite dim and dark inside the hut. It smelled musty and damp, and shivering a little, Randy began to look around. Jinnicky was tapping the bricks about the fireplace, examining the clock and broken vases on the mantel, picking up the fire tongs, shovel and hearth broom—for any of these objects might easily be the King and his family.

253

"If I just had a bit more light," he murmured discontentedly, "I might be able to see what I am about. Are there any lamps or candles around, my boy?" Randy, with the same idea in mind, had searched both rooms on the first floor and now, feeling his way up the rickety steps, he looked carefully in the two rooms above. But there was not a candle, match or lamp to be found.

"How about lighting a fire?" he proposed, coming back to the hearth where Jinnicky was squinting earnestly at the iron fender. "Only we have no matches," he added ruefully.

"Pooh, I can easily start a fire with my red incense. Fetch the red bottle, Randy, and be quick, be quick, or the Wizard of Oz will be stealing a march on us and working his magic before I have a chance to try mine." The fire was all ready to start and pushing the donkey out of the way, Randy, following Jinnicky's instructions, sprinkled the red incense over the kindling and logs and snapped his fingers four times. The paper and kindling caught at once and as Randy seized the poker to adjust the logs better, an ear-piercing scream went up the chimney. Dropping the poker, Randy fell against Jinnicky, and small wonder! The end of the first log to catch fire was changing to a face, the frightened face of Pumper, the King's Prime Minister! As Randy and the Jinn looked on in horror, the King's head crackled merrily from the end of the second log, and his royal feet, esconced in purple boots, beat a wild tattoo on the log underneath.

"Oh! Oh! Oh!" shrieked Randy, hopping from one foot to the other. "They'll be burned up. Jinnicky, Jinnicky! What'll we do? Where's some water? Wait, I'll go for some water!" But Jinnicky, seizing Randy by both wrists held him fast.

"They're not burning," spluttered the Red Jinn breathlessly. "Be still! Stay here! If you put out that fire they'll have to stay part logs and part people forever. The only way to restore people who have been turned to wood is to burn the wood."

"But this is awful!" choked the Gilliken boy, trying his best to pull away. And awful indeed it was to see the half logs and half people crackling and blazing away in Faleero's grate. Pumper had stopped screaming and the others, making no sound at all, stared with solemn eyes through the flames at the two figures on the hearth.

"How long will it take?" gasped Randy. "Oh, Jinnicky, can't you hurry it up a little? I can't bear it!" Jinnicky did not answer but dropped Randy's wrists and opening his eyes, which for the moment he had shut tight, Randy saw King Pompus gravely helping the Queen over the fender; Prince Pompadore and Peg Amy with the baby princess in her arms came next, and last of all, Pumper, looking terribly frightened and ill at ease. They were still smoking but seemed perfectly comfortable.

"How can I ever thank you?" wheezed the King, seizing the Red Jinn by both shoulders and embracing him heartily.

"Thank him!" cried Jinnicky, waving his arm at Randy. "He started the fire, so he is really responsible for your disenchantment."

"Why, it's the little grape eater!" exclaimed Pompus, turning to Randy in honest surprise. "Well, well, and well! Give me your hand, young one."

"Oh, do tell us what happened!" begged the Queen. "I remember nothing since picking the fire rose, but I am sure some great misfortune has befallen."

"I told you not to pick those flowers," muttered Prince Pompadore, shaking the ashes out of his pockets. "I'll wager that traveling magician was at the bottom of the whole business."

"Where's Kabumpo? I want to hear the rest of

the story about the pink goat," wailed Pajonia, blinking sleepily over her mother's shoulder.

"There's more than one story to be told, my child," sniffed Jinnicky, rolling his red glass eyes solemnly from one to the other. "And if your Highnesses will be seated, I will endeavor to tell you all, or a small part of all that has happened."

So, regardless of dust and grime, the royal family of Pumperdink sat down on the wooden benches beside the still smouldering fire and Jinnicky proceeded to tell them of Faleero's wickedness and Kettywig's treachery.

"And you came all the way from Ev to help us," mused Peg Amy, smiling at the rosy little Jinn. "What ever can we do to repay you? Why, you and Randy and Kabumpo have saved the whole kingdom."

"Don't forget Johnwan," piped up Randy. "Oh say, Jinnicky, I've just thought of something. Lend me your looking glasses, quick!" Without waiting for Jinnicky to say yes, Randy pulled the specs from the Red Jinn's nose and ran hurriedly out of the cabin.

"My mercy me! Stop him! Stop him!" cried Jinnicky, running round in a frenzied circle. "The boy's gone after that great wooden soldier and will be lost, destroyed or stolen. Oh! Oh! Oh! He's the best and only boy friend I have ever had." But by the time they reached the door Randy had disappeared. Pretending to search for him further, Pumper, who was heartily ashamed of himself and anxious to escape before the King got round to his

case, slipped into the forest running as fast and as far as he could. Where he went, I have no idea. I only know he was never heard of or seen in Pumperdink again, and as Kabumpo often remarked to Pompus, a grumpy good thing it was, too!

258

Without noticing the disappearance of the Prime Pumper, the King and his family and the Red Jinn decided to return to the palace. Placing Queen Pozy, Princess Peg Amy and Pajonia on the donkey, the King and Prince Pompadore and Jinnicky set out on foot through the forest. The King led the donkey; Prince Pompadore and Jinnicky walked together, Pompa carrying the heavy wicker baskets, and so happy were they all to be released from the wicked enchantments that they scarcely noticed the inconveniences of walking. But it took a long, long time and it was almost night when they finally reached the castle.

Lights blazed from every window and while the Wizard feverishly tried one spell after another, the servants were preparing a great feast to celebrate their Majesties' return. Kabumpo had assured them that the Wizard of Oz would produce the royal family in time for dinner, and when the chief footman saw them wearily mounting the castle steps he gave a loud cheer for the Wizard and forgetting his dignity —also his decorum—hugged the King, kissed the donkey and dashed into the palace to break the wonderful news to the others. So, as the little procession moved toward the throne room, Ozma and her councillors rushed out of the dining hall, and followed by the courtiers and servants, completely surrounded the little party.

"Three cheers for the Wizard of Oz!" they shouted hysterically. "Three cheers for the Wizard!"

"Wizard!" cried Jinnicky indignantly. "The Wizard had nothing to do with it. 'Twas Randy, this honest mountain lad, who turned the trick and released their Royal Highnesses!"

"Ah, but you all have helped us," put in Queen Pozy, tactfully sliding off the donkey and holding both hands out to the Sovereign of all Oz.

"We never, never, *never* can thank you enough! And if it had not been for Kabumpo, where would we have been by now?" The Elegant Elephant looked pleased but self-conscious and after the whole family had shaken his trunk and the little princess had blown him three kisses, he suddenly missed Randy.

"Where's the boy?" he asked, and picking Jinnicky up in his trunk he stared anxiously into his eyes. "Speak up! Speak up, can't you?"

"How am I to speak any other way?" grinned the little Jinn, making swimming motions in the air. "Put me down, El, there's a good fellow."

"But what happened?" asked Dorothy.

OZMA AND HER COUNCILLORS RUSHED OUT OF THE DINING HALL

261

"Yes, how did a young lad, unpracticed in magic, succeed where all our art failed?" demanded the Wizard of Oz in a peppery voice.

"Chance! Pure chance," murmured Jinnicky, winking a red glass eye at the Wizard. "Your magic

is not very swift, my dear Wiz, not so swift as I was led to suppose."

"Now! Now!" put in the Scarecrow, wagging his crooked finger at the Jinn. "Green magic may not be as swift as red magic, but it's far prettier!"

"Where's Randy?" roared Kabumpo, giving Jinnicky an impatient shake.

"Gone off with my magic glasses to find the wooden soldier," announced Jinnicky ruefully. "My mercy me, El, we'll have to go after him at once! If your Highnesses will excuse us—" Jinnicky took off his lid and bowed as well as he could in his precarious position. The King, not to be outdone, took off his crown and while Kabumpo, still holding Jinnicky in his trunk, simply dashed out of the throne room, Prince Pompadore explained to his curious listeners all that had happened in Faleero's hut.

"Where shall we look first?" demanded Kabumpo, plunging down the steps of the castle two at a time. "Great Grump, what's this?" A huge figure, so covered with mud and water weeds as to be entirely indistinguishable, stepped stiffly across the courtyard. Beside him trudged the Gilliken boy whistling cheerily and unconcernedly.

"Randy! Randy, my boy, how did you get back so soon?"

"Back?" called Randy in surprise. "Why, I never went away." Clicking the instrument that controlled Johnwan, he brought the muddy warrior to a neat halt before his two comrades. "I just put on Jinnicky's specs and asked them to find Johnwan's signal," explained Randy eagerly. "I ran away from Faleero's hut and the looking glasses brought me right to this terrace, and pressed in the gold dust between the flags I discovered the controller."

"Then what?" asked Jinnicky.

"Why, then," continued Randy, in a matter of fact voice, "thinking Johnwan might have fallen, I gave him the signal to rise, face about and march home. And you see it worked, for here he is!"

"Very good!" approved Jinnicky. "Get a hose!"

"That won't be necessary," rumbled Kabumpo. Setting Jinnicky on the ground he waddled over to the fountain, filled his trunk with water and gave Johnwan several complete and cleansing showers. Soon all the mud was washed away, and the wooden soldier, a bit worse for wear and tear and with the unconscious Faleero still under his arm, emerged.

"Well, I hope this will be a lesson to her," muttered Jinnicky severely. "I'll bet Johnwan has walked on the bottom of a dozen lakes."

"But what shall we do with her now?" demanded Randy worriedly. "She may come to any minute."

"Oh, let the King decide," sniffed the Red Jinn airily. "We've done our share and I'm hungry!"

CHAPTER 20

"The Purple Prince Has Earned His Crown!"

JOHNWAN, in spite of his washed out appearance, caused a real sensation when he stalked into the throne room with Faleero, who had recovered her senses, screaming and kicking under his arm. Ozma, always quick to think and act, immediately touched her magic belt and before the old fairy could cause further mischief or unhappiness turned her to a raven. Croaking with fright and anger Faleero flew out of the window and that was the last anyone ever saw or heard of the Princess of Follensby Forest. The three old ladies in waiting had already fled back to the hut in the clearing. Kettywig, after a stern lecture, had been sent home, and so, in complete possession of his crown, his kingdom, his family and his castle, Pompus proudly led his distinguished guests and rescuers into dinner.

The cook who had been turned into a cocoanut pie —which, fortunately, nobody had eaten—had been restored by Ozma to his proper shape; also the four guardsmen, so that all was as before and everyone was happy and content.

Now there have been many feasts and celebrations in the palace of Pumperdink, but the feast celebrating the restoration of the lost sovereigns surpassed them all. The chefs had truly outdone themselves and the jolly red face of Jinnicky, who was seated between the prince and princess, shone with enjoyment and satisfaction. Beside the King at the head of the table sat Ozma of Oz and Randy. On either side of the Queen, at the foot, sat The Wizard of Oz and Dorothy. The Scarecrow was next to Princess Pajonia and she crowed with delight at his droll tricks and stories. Johnwan stood stiffly at attention behind Randy's chair and Kabumpo, after swallowing three bales of hay and a dozen buckets of peanuts, ambled round the table laughing and joking with everyone.

The King and his courtiers could not hear enough of the strange adventures of Randy, the Elegant Elephant and the Red Jinn, and all over and in great detail Kabumpo told the entire story. The Scarecrow was highly interested in the Guide Post Man and meant to hunt him up at his first opportunity. Ozma was curious to learn all about the Double King, while Nandywog, the little giant, pleased Dorothy best of all. The Wizard, after noting in his green memorandum book the exact location of Torpedo Town, got into a lively argument with Jinnicky about red magic. They had quite forgotten their professional jealousies and while each realized that without Jinnicky's looking glasses little could have been done, as Randy had actually brought about the release of the Royal Family, neither felt that he had triumphed over the other, and in consequence they were fast becoming friends. Indeed, by ice cream and cake time, there was such a feeling of good fellowship and jollity that the very candles seemed to jig in their holders. Even the solemn-faced footmen forgot their pomposity and importance and joined boisterously in the singing of Pumperdink's National Air.

After the last note had died away, Pompus rose

with as much dignity as his happiness and weight would permit and offered Randy a permanent home in the palace with the title of Younger Prince of the Realm. At this the cheering was deafening, Kabumpo trumpeting his approval above all the rest.

But before Randy could accept, Jinnicky bounced to his feet and declared that Randy was to return with him. He intended to make him his sole heir, sharer of his magic formulas and ruler after him in his mighty dominions in Ev. Ozma and Dorothy smiled sympathetically and the whole company in breathless interest waited for the mountain boy to make his choice. But he never did, for as he stood up and bowed first to the King and then to Jinnicky, there came a loud and sudden crash and in through the shattered glass of the long window behind the King shot two thin and excited old gentlemen. The first wore a tall, pointed cap and a long cloak covered with stars and moons. The second was dressed in purple satin knee breeches and doublet with a fine three-cornered hat. He carried a velvet cushion on which there blazed a tall and splendid crown of amethyst. The royal diners and celebrities were too astonished to move or speak, but the gentleman in the three-cornered hat promptly saved them that trouble. Skipping over to Randy, he called out in a high, trembling voice:

"The Prince of the Purple Mountain has earned his crown and won his Kingdom! Randywell, Handy-well, Brandenburg Bompadoo, I hereby crown you

269

King of Regalia and all the Regalians! Long live King Randy!" Placing the crown on Randy's head, Hoochafoo, for it *was* Hoochafoo, as you have guessed all along, embraced his nephew so heartily that the crown fell off and rolled under the table.

"A King!" coughed Kabumpo, falling against a pillar. "And to think he once fastened my collars. Great Grump! I said he was no common mountain boy." While the company recovered from their surprise and amazement as best they could, a footman hastily restored Randy's crown, and Jinnicky, bounding out of his chair, was the first to congratulate the new ruler.

"I liked you from the very first," declared the Red Jinn, clapping Randy on the back and then embracing him affectionately. "And remember, if you ever tire of your own kingdom you can always have half of mine!"

"And mine!" boomed Pompus heartily.

"And mine," echoed little Princess Pajonia, waving her golden spoon.

"But tell us, how did you come here?" begged Ozma, turning curiously to the wise man. "And tell us how Randy happened to be disguised and why he came to Pumperdink in the first place?"

"We came by the magic of the amethyst ball," answered Chalulu impressively. "In Regalia, a kingdom of which your Highness may have heard, it is the law that when the King shall disappear, retire or cease to rule, his son shall go forth on a journey of adventure and alone and without help prove his

fitness to receive the crown. Without knowing the conditions of this scroll," Chalulu raised the long parchment roll in one hand, "the Prince must fulfill all its tests. When this is done, the amethyst ball in the palace transports me, the oldest wise man

271

and the oldest member of the King's family, to the exact spot where he happens to be. Each time his Highness fulfilled a condition of the test, the ball flashed fire. Seven flashes told us he had successfully passed them all and the eighth flash brought us to this strange imperial palace." Chalulu bowed to King Pompus, then to Queen Pozy and then to all of the others. "And here we are happy to find our young King in a distinguished company of friends and celebrities."

"Oh, yes!" Randy assured him quickly. "I shall hate to leave here, uncle."

"What were those conditions you were talking about?" asked Kabumpo, in a muffled voice to hide his grief at losing Randy. The very thought of the separation made the poor elephant choke and sputter.

"Well," sniffed the wise man, who enjoyed being the center of attention. "Suppose I read them."

A chair was brought for Uncle Hoochafoo and while all the others resumed their seats, the wise man read the conditions from the royal scroll of Regalia. Randy was perhaps the most interested listener, for though he knew he must prove himself in seven ways, he had not known the nature of the tests he must pass at all.

"The prince," began Chalulu, looking benevolently at Randy over his specs, "must first make three true friends."

"Kabumpo was the first," said the boy, putting his arm around the Elegant Elephant's trunk, for Kabumpo had come to stand right beside him. "And I suppose Nandywog was the second. Jinnicky certainly was the third, but now I have hundreds!" He glanced proudly down the long table and with smiles, nods and approving cheers the gay company assured him that he had.

"Second, the prince must serve a strange King," announced Chalulu, when at last the cheering had died away.

"I was the King, but I am a strange King no longer. You certainly served me, my boy, served me right!" Placing his hand on Randy's shoulder, Pompus beamed at Regalia's newly crowned sovereign.

"Third, he must save a Queen," continued the wise man in a calm voice.

"I was the Queen." Waving her silk handkerchief, Pozy nodded happily at her rescuer.

"Fourth, the prince must prove his bravery in battle," read Chalulu without looking up.

"Pooh, he proved his bravery dozens and dozens of times," trumpeted Kabumpo proudly, "but the first and best was when he caught that bundle of blazing twigs and threw them back at Faleero."

"Fifth, ahem—fifth!" Chalulu cleared his throat and waited a few minutes for silence, "fifth, the prince must overcome a fabulous monster."

"Well, he did that, too," cried Jinnicky. "Upon the combinoceros he fell and saved himself and us!"

"Sixth, the prince must disenchant a princess," continued Chalulu imperturbably.

"He did more than that," Peg Amy assured them, holding little princess Pajonia high in her arms. "He disenchanted two princesses and a prince, so three cheers for Randywell, Handywell, Brandenburg Bompadoo!"

"And lastly," finished the wise man, as Randy, overcome by embarrassment, got behind Kabumpo, "lastly, he must receive from a wizard some important magic treasure."

"Oh, that's Johnwan!" exclaimed Randy coming out eagerly. "Look, Uncle Hoochafoo, this great wooden soldier is mine. Jinnicky gave him to me and as soon as he copies him for his own army, he's coming to Regalia to be my bodyguard."

"Dear, dear, dear!" murmured Uncle Hoochafoo, drawing out his monocle and eyeing Johnwan dubiously. "Is this a magic treasure?"

"Of course! Of course!" Clicking Johnwan's control, Randy made him face about, march and salute

and even the wise man had to admit the points and excellence of the wooden warrior. By the time the excitement following the crowning of Randy and the reading of the scroll had died down, by the time the wise man and Hoochafoo had been told the story

275

of the new King's adventures, the clock in the great tower had tolled two, and in spite of their interest and thankfulness the company began to yawn and blink with weariness. Pompus begged all his royal visitors to spend not only the night but a week in his palace. Ozma, however, had important matters to settle in the Emerald City next day and after expressing her happiness and delight at the satisfactory way everything had turned out, she left on a fast wish with Dorothy, the Wizard, Jack and the Scarecrow. Randy would dearly have loved to stay, but his uncle and the wise man, feeling that the formal coronation must take place at once, insisted that they must leave immediately for Regalia.

"My mercy me!" sniffed Jinnicky, shaking hands and then clasping the boy King to his shiny bosom. "How ever am I to get along without you? Will you come to see the old man soon and often?"

"I certainly will," promised Randy, pressing Jinnicky's plump hand. Then, to keep from breaking down, he pointed a mischievous finger at Jinnicky's head. "Why, Jinnicky," he murmured in a scandalized voice, "you need a hair cut!"

"Ha, ha! Hee, hee! That's what Alibabble will be telling me," blubbered the Red Jinn, pretending to laugh so hard that he cried, but really crying so hard he couldn't laugh. Kabumpo felt even worse, for he had known Randy longer. Not trusting himself to speak the boy gave Kabumpo a huge hug. Then, lifting one of the Elegant Elephant's enormous ears he whispered hurriedly:

"Never mind, as soon as I'm crowned I'll run away and come back. As—" But before he could finish, Chalulu, who was terribly weary, touched the amethyst ball he had under his arm and seizing Randy by one hand and the purple-bearded uncle by the other, flashed out of sight and Pumperdink.

"Well, sniff, sniff!" The Red Jinn sobbed unashamedly, leaning against Kabumpo. "He's gone, and all our good times with him! My mercy me! I'd set my heart on taking him home with me!"

"Never you mind," wheezed Kabumpo, patting Jinnicky hard on the back with his trunk. "There's no law against visiting. And if your Highness will, and *can* spare me, I've a notion to spend three months of every year in Regalia with Randywell, Handywell, Brandenburg Bompadoo!"

"Hear! Hear!" chuckled Pompus indulgently. "Well, under the circumstances, old fellow, we shall have to allow it."

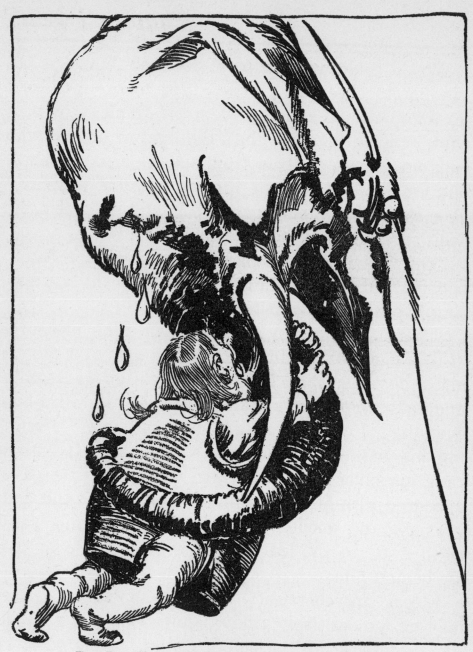

THE RED JINN SOBBED, LEANING AGAINST KABUMPO
278

Why, I could do that, too," declared Jinnicky, beginning to cheer up a little. "My mercy me, we'll go together! Of course," went on Jinnicky, with a wink at King Pompus, "he's the kind of animal who calls an orange a citrus fruit and a porch a piazza, but I'm kind of fond of the big begonia anyway." The Red Jinn, amid roars of laughter, shook his head several times to prove this statement.

"You're not such a bad little fellow yourself!" boomed Kabumpo, taking off Jinnicky's lid and setting it back slightly askew.

"Thanks!" Jinnicky smiled with real pleasure. "I'll be back for you in a month and a day. A month and a day, remember! Then off we'll go to Regalia and take Johnwan to Randy. Good-bye! Good-bye everyone! I've had a magnificus time here." Hanging his baskets on Johnwan's arm, the Red Jinn rang his silver dinner bell, and when the little slave appeared with his tray, Jinnicky seized his hand and grasping the wooden soldier by the coat tails vanished away to Ev, leaving not even a ripple in the air behind him.

"Great gooseberries! These disappearances are making me positively giddy," gulped the King, staring ruefully at all the empty chairs. "How quiet it will seem in the palace without that Jinn. Ho, hum! What a day! What a day! And it's already to-morrow and after I've had a nap I'll have to think of some fitting way to reward Randy and this Red Jinn for their trouble."

"You, my dear General," Pompus turned to General Quakes, who was yawning in a well-bred fashion behind his hand, "you shall be Prime Minister as well as commander of my army and have Pumper's place and salary besides, for I do not believe we ever will see that old rascal again." General Quakes bowed to show his appreciation and as Kabumpo, on his way to bed, affectionately touched the King on the shoulder, Pompus seized his old friend and adviser firmly by the trunk.

"What shall we do for you?" he asked eagerly. "I promise, Kabumpo, you shall have anything your heart desires!" Kabumpo nodded absently, for now that Randy was gone he could think of nothing he wanted. Calling drowsy good-nights and good wishes the royal family and courtiers and servants went yawning to bed to dream of magic transformations, strange journeys and monsters. But Kabumpo had the best dream of all. With Randy and the little Red Jinn on his back, with Johnwan marching sturdily before, Kabumpo dreamed he was climbing the purple mountains of Regalia.

And when Kabumpo's dream does come true— when the Elegant Elephant and Jinnicky really go to visit Randy in Regalia—that, my dears, will be another book and another story!